Corrugated Roads.
Rollin' down the Road.
1960s-1970s.

G. Dixon Lowndes

About Corrugated Roads…

Once upon a time the Jae family lived in a tiny drought-stricken desert town that was miles from anywhere in The Outback of Australia in the nineteen fifties. Growing up in it was covered in the first volume of this series, *Corrugated Roads. A Bugger of a Kid. 1950s-1960s.*

During the 1960s-1970s, Jenny Jae continues to chronicle her rough and tumble experiences that began with life in an alcoholic family and town, finding shelter and sobriety in a vibrant Aboriginal community, being schooled by the Sisters of Mercy who had none and striking out on her own.

Jenny soon discovers that life doesn't always go the way she thought it would and she has to scramble to survive especially in the dangerous duality of family and suburbia.

Two eminent Australian writers, Alan Marshall (I Can Jump Puddles) and Geoffrey Dean (Mysteries, Myths and Miracles) said:

Corrugated Roads is a gritty telling, and a book that I couldn't put down. And, in spite of its serious subject matter, there is relief in the unexpected humour that arises out of the girl's imaginative misconceptions about events beyond her experience.
Geoffrey Dean, Writer.

Her wealth of experience would be the envy of any writer wanting to write an epic about the life of an Australian girl she is a long way ahead of her time. Her stories are amazingly varied but tying them all together is a natural understanding of human character and a keen eye to record the significant: these are extremely modern and frank stories.
Alan Marshall. Writer.

G. Dixon Lowndes is an award winning Australian author who has written for television (Neighbours) as well as print (Playboy).

Published by Ginny Lowndes
PO Box 957
Cabramatta NSW 2166
Web: http://www.ginnylowndes.com

Corrugated Roads is told so far through three novels:

Corrugated Roads. A Bugger of a Kid. 1950s-1960s.
Published by Montpelier Press. 2010. Create Space. 2015.
Corrugated Roads. Rolling Down the Road. 1960s-1970s.
Published by Create Space. 2015.
Corrugated Roads. Lilies on a Dustbin. 1970s-1980s.
Published by Create Space. 2015.

Apart from use permitted under the Copyright Act 1968 and subsequent amendments, no part of this publication may be reproduced, stored in a retrieval system or transmitted by any means or process whatsoever without the permission of the copyright holder and publisher, Ginny Dixon Lowndes. A CIP catalogue record for this title is available from the National Library of Australia.

Manuscripts and other material by Ginny Lowndes are housed at The John Oxley Library, State Library of Queensland. Reference Code 10147.

OUT OF THE BLUE

As dawn swirled through the sky splashing rose gold, pink and lemon into the blue around me, the fruit pickers stirred in their swags. The sun scattered the stars. Birds flitted in and out of blue–grey leaves.

On a branch a large pair of ravens try to intimidate everyone smaller than they were with their slow "Ah, ah, aaah, aaaaaah". Tiny mynah birds declared war on them. They launched themselves from a branch and pierced their bright yellow beaks into the ravens' soft brownish-black underbelly. After dozens of small sharp spears struck their stomachs the ravens flew away.

The blue on blue on blue day'd begun and the sun'd started to roast everything and everybody in it. As I splashed my face in the cool water from the cattle trough I listened to the sounds of the bush and any potential danger in it. As a child I'd spent a lot of time in one silent order of nuns or other listening and anticipating. I'd gone blind from allergies and the nuns'd told my parents they could fix it for them. For years, each time Mum and Dad dragged me from the house to the overnight train to go back to the convents I was torn to pieces with grief, dread and heart-thumping terror.

By the time I'd left school everything about me had a nervous quickness—my movements, my abilities, my mind and my instant obedience to terrifying adults that allowed me to escape as soon as I could.

'You never put money into a girl,' Dad used to tell all and sundry. 'They just go off and marry someone else and his family git all the benefit. Nothin' in it for me. Never invest in anything that eats.' My parents told me I could make my own way in life without any help from them so I hit the road. I was fifteen.

One day, I told myself as I trudged down the road, when I've got enough money I'm going back to the city to study music. I'll become a writer and write what I need to write. I will not cost anyone anything. I will pay for myself. I will never ever ask anyone for anything. Meantime I had to eat and earn enough to pay for it. My current job was to pick late summer crops. At night I slept near some itinerant women for protection. In the morning I'd have a dingo's for breakfast.

I lived frugally and saved what I could. Besides I was only paid half a male wage for the same work they did so I didn't have much. I wasn't allowed to have a bank account unless I was vouched for by a man so I tied what spare change I had in a handkerchief and pinned it inside the pocket of my one and only pair of Levis. Out on the road I'd never let anyone know if I was frightened, hurt, lonely or in need. Not if I could help it. I'd rather be caught dead than thought weak or whinging, and sometimes I'd risk the former to avoid the latter.

Unfairness of any kind towards other people incensed me immediately and mortal combat over injustice came easy. I told myself I'd always speak to all the people I met as one human being to another because so few spoke like that to me. At night as I watched the stars I decided I'd only own what I could carry and let my footprints blow away in the wurlie wind.

One day, out of the blue, Mum got hold of me through the stock and station agency that represented Grandfather's cattle property. She wanted to invite me back home so we could celebrate my sixteenth birthday together.

'As a family,' she said.

You can't go back. You can't. They told you to get out, that they didn't want you.

'It'll be such fun, Jennifer.'

Mum always called me by my full name. When people called me J, or Jen or Jenny, she corrected them before denouncing them as lower class and not worth knowing. Right now though, Mum was saying everything I'd always wanted to hear.

'I've booked the local hall and invited all your friends to come.'

What friends?

'Some of the boys have formed a band so we can play records and dance.'

You always told me I was too tall and ungainly to be seen dancing.

"How on earth you're going to find anyone to marry you is beyond me," she'd say. "And stop smiling or at least cover your mouth when you feel one coming on. You have the worst mouth and teeth I've ever seen. The best thing for you to do is not to draw attention to yourself." Other times she'd say, "Good luck with that face."

I'd tried to remain short, unsmiling and invisible but as Mum talked I began to finger the coins in my pocket.

They were expecting me to come in on the train but I'd hitchhiked down the Warrego Highway to save money. Uncle Charlie, one of Dad's black brothers'd picked me up outside Roma. My heart beat loudly in the excitement and terror at being back home again.

Uncle Lincoln was sitting under the Tree of Knowledge outside the newsagency. His white shirt was crisp and his brown trousers had a knife–edge crease in them. His black face was shaded by a spotless white cowboy hat sitting low on his forehead. He was deep in conversation with his brother, Uncle Lionel. Ethel McPherson, Lionel's girlfriend, was window–shopping nearby. They'd been together for years now. "Without the benefit of marriage," Mum'd add darkly whenever they were mentioned.

Blackfellas had their own way of marrying and they didn't need a church, Uncle Lincoln said. He was the only one who had time for me as a little kid. He told me he could always see me coming to The Mish because invisible sparks shot out of me from all sides. It made me look like a small indignant fireball.

I caught sight of myself in the cabin mirror of Uncle Charlie's truck. My face had fine yet sharply defined features, blue eyes and a fair smattering of freckles. I'd also headed towards six feet despite my best efforts. I wore jeans, brown work boots and a white long–sleeved shirt with my reddish-gold hair tucked up under a brown checked cap.

After Uncle Charlie dropped me off just before the One Mile Creek he'd tooted his horn and waved as he drove away. He'd told me to tell Dad he'd see him at the races. Dad always lost at the races.

I swung my swag up on my shoulder and walked towards home. The north-westerly wind blistered down the road. The trees made a half-hearted attempt to rustle its leaves in it.

Is Thrippy in there somewhere?

Mum'd made Dad get rid of Baby Girl's cat once. It took two years to walk back home after Dad dumped it down near St George. Baby Girl'd devoted herself to it and its limp for the rest of its life. I hoped Thrippy would come home one day too. I didn't believe Henry shot her.

All around me the earth'd fractured into giant dry chocolate chips. I couldn't resist jumping on them to hear them crack and crunch under my feet the way they'd done when I was a kid. The old pise house seemed to've shrunk as it'd tried to ward off the heat.

Everything seemed to've grown smaller.

I pushed the rusty front gate open and walked down the crunchy gravel path. It was still lined with exhausted geraniums. Their leaves gasped towards the ground. Dogs began to bark.

The front door was locked. No one locked a door out here. I knocked loudly. There was no reply. I walked around the verandah to try to get some windows open but they too were shut all bar one. As I tried to climb through it someone grabbed me from behind. I spun around, hit them with a flurry of fists so hard in the stomach and jaw that they fell on the floorboards. My cap'd come off and my hair'd flown around my shoulders.

'Jennifer! What on earth do you think you're doing?'

'I was trying to get in when he jumped me.' I pointed to my brother Henry who lay on the verandah, winded.

'Are you alright, Henry?' Mum'd come quickly up the verandah.

'Yair, terrific.'

I put my hand out to lever him up. 'Sorry Henry.' I only made half an apology. 'You never did keep your guard up properly.'

'I just didn't recognise you that's all.'

'Bet you would've had second thoughts if you had.'

Mum was furious. 'I don't see that it's anything to boast about, Jennifer. Your father ought to be ashamed of himself—teaching a girl how to box.'

'Well Henry wasn't interested.' I was determined to stick up for myself. 'Aren't you pleased to see me Mum?'

'Of course I am.' Her voice was as limp as a dishrag. 'I wasn't expecting to see you until the weekend. How did you get here?'

I stuck my cap back on and swung my swag jauntily over my shoulder. 'I hitched.'

'You what?' Mum glanced around the bare acreages near our house looking for neighbours who might've been able to see or hear what was going on.

'Uncle Charlie gave me a lift in one of his trucks.'

I'd begun to lose my footing.

'Charlie Smith is a no–hoper.' Mum dismissed him and me with a toss of her head. She hated all Dad's relatives and wanted to get as far away from them as possible.

'He is not.'

Uncle Charlie worked as a wood carter and a mechanic. When Dad and his brother Uncle Rhodie were kids they'd had a ringbarking team with Uncle Charlie and his brother. His son was showing great promise as a footballer. With the ball under his arm, he usually strolled over the line with the rest of the footballers hanging off him like bunting.

'Every one of his children has been in trouble with the law. Or so I've heard.'

'They have not. Besides,' I couldn't help myself, 'it happens in the best of families; more if you're black. The Bullymen are always picking on them. They're lovely people. The police should leave them alone. They're highly respectable.' I tried to think of something to change the subject. 'You haven't changed a bit.' I tried to keep my voice in as friendly a tone as I could without smiling.

'And neither have you by the look of it.' Mum's face was as black as thunder. 'The first thing you're going to do is take a shower and get out of those clothes. No wonder Henry thought you were a boy.'

'That's why I tackled her.'

Henry'd grown much taller than me over the past year or so. He reminded me of someone I'd met before. His lanky build ended in tousled red curls tufted on top of his head. He too was as blue–eyed and as freckled as me.

Mum'd sent him out into the bush with some carpenters as an apprentice but I'd heard from one of Uncle Lincoln's mob I met while I going from town to town that he'd run away and walked a hundred miles or so back home.

His bowel was still dangling out of his body when he got there, he'd added somewhat mysteriously. It'd become severely infected. Gran'd eventually got him to a doctor and looked after him but no one spoke about it or said why Henry's bowel had managed to end up dangling out of his body. Nothing ever happened to us. No matter what happened. It was always nothing.

Mum got some keys out to open the front door. The burnished brown hallway suggested that Uncle Lincoln's sister, Auntie Pearl was still doing the cleaning.

My piano stood against the lounge room wall surrounded by big old tapestry chairs. Despite Sister Mary Catherine smashing the piano lid down on my hands when I made a mistake or beating me with her leather belt I still wanted to create beautiful sounds in it. To keep practising on the road I used to draw a keyboard in the dirt and go over and over the music in my head on it.

Mum turned the key in the back door lock. 'Go and get your sister.'

Henry ran down the steps towards the woodheap. Baby Girl sat on an old log in the boiling heat. Henry beckoned her to come inside and then walked back up the stairs into the kitchen.

That's who he reminds me of. The piano player in The Valley. The Fairy Man.

Mum filled the kettle with some water and put it on the stove. Her creamy blouse was tucked into a brown, figure hugging calf–length sheath skirt. Her feet were encased in dark brown stiletto sandals. Her small waist was highlighted with a gold and brown belt. The Marcel waves in her chestnut hair fell around her face. Despite it all, the walls seemed cold and dark as if shadows had crept in to steal her sunlight.

Baby Girl slouched towards the stairs in old shorts and a tattered shirt. She sat down on the steps and began to remove her shoes. At least I thought that was what she was doing.

Mum caught me looking at her. Her green eyes gleamed with a malice that said if you've been stupid enough and boofheaded enough to fall for the bait I've put out, I'm entitled to switch it into something else and laugh at you for trusting me. Just seeing me reinforced her belief that I wasn't quite all there. A few sandwiches short of a picnic she'd tell people as she repeated the story-of-the-stick to make her point.

'Get into the shower. And try to fix that face of yours up. You're as plain as a pikestaff. Pity you take after your father's side of the family. A real Plain Jane aren't you? And for God's sake try to change into something decent while you're at it.'

Henry snickered.

You'll keep.

I picked up my swag, walked over to the bathroom and shut the door. All I could change into was more of the same. I'd left a few clothes my city cousins had given me hidden in what used to be my bedroom. I didn't know if they'd fit anymore or even if they were still there. I sat in the darkened room on the side of the white tub. My stomach felt queasy. My brain wouldn't work. I gasped for breath. My heart was beating out of my chest then it began to twist. I put a little water in a mug to wash the dust out of my throat. I rinsed myself under the red gritty dirt water that came out of the tap.

I shouldn't have come back. I shouldn't have believed her. I should've known.

After I towelled myself quickly I changed into clean jeans and a plain black t–shirt. As I tied my hair back in a ponytail I could hear Mum and Dad talking.

'Who's blockin' up the bathroom?'

'Ing, Tom, ing. It's Jennifer.' Mum was still correcting Dad's use of the English language by adding the 'ings' onto everything he deliberately dropped off.

'Thought she wasn't due for a few more days.'

Mum clattered around the stove. 'You ought to be shot.'

'What—again?'

'She punched Henry in the stomach.'

'Soft enough landin'.'

Dad was geeing Mum up into a fury.

'Ing! Ing!' Mum's voice shook in rage. 'That'd be right. Stick up for everyone except your own son. And you wonder why the two of you don't get on.'

I opened the door. 'Hello Dad. The bathroom's free if you want it.'

'Gidday Jen.' Dad poured himself a rum. He caught me looking at it. 'Back's playin' up again.'

We eyed each other awkwardly. Dad drummed his fingers on the table. Our family never showed the slightest bit of affection toward each other.

'Jennifer.' Mum corrected Dad again as she sucked on a cigarette. 'I loathe people shortening perfectly good names. Her name, Tom, is Jennifer. I'd like you all to call her that from now on.'

If you do I'll flatten you. I'm Jenny or Jen. I refuse to be a Jennifer.

Mum stubbed out one cigarette to light another. She'd tried grog when she was younger but she'd blacked out after each attempt. She had no idea what she'd done in those twenty–four hour periods. It'd scared her so much that now she only smoked and drank tea. She never ate much either.

'Don't you have anything better to wear?' Mum turned her attention back to me. 'You look like a hobo—something you'd find in a gutter.'

Baby Girl was sitting at the kitchen table. She had hessian bags tied around her feet. She'd grown thinner and whiter. Her straw yellow hair was chopped into a short back and sides. Even though I said hello a couple of times she didn't look up.

Blood trickled from one her of the fingernails she'd bitten in to.

'You'd better move that horse of yours up to the home paddock, BG.' Dad told her after she sat down.

'Belinda Gemma. Call her by her right name.' Mum was hissing her words now. 'It's Belinda.' She didn't want the neighbours to hear.

Mum's brother was also called Thomas so Dad was called Tom to avoid confusion. He was the exception to the naming rule. Baby Girl got up to do as she was told. She sat down on the back steps to remove the hessian bags before she went down the back paddock.

Dad continued to drum his fingers on the table. 'She's in the Pony Club. Jake puts them through their paces.' Dad paused before he continued baiting Mum. 'She's always been good with a horse that Jake.'

Mum snapped at the bait. 'I can't stand the rotten things. They set my teeth on edge. And her name's Jacqueline, Tom, not Jake. Why do all the women out here want to be like men?' She shuddered before she turned on me. 'Well that hair of yours could do with a good cut. Long hair doesn't suit you whatsoever. Makes you look bovine.' She loudly over–pronounced the French hairdresser's name so it could be heard in Paris. 'You can go up to Violetta later on. She'll do it without an appointment as a favour to me.' Mum smiled at her brush with a foreign culture and her influence. 'I've got some clothes in a rag bag in the laundry. You can go through them later to see if you can find anything to fit you.'

From the tone in her voice I could tell she doubted I'd be able to get my foot into anything let alone the rest of me. "You're just too fat," she'd always say after I'd tried.

"Just lie doggo," Uncle Lincoln whispered in my head from a long time ago. "Listen and learn, bubby, listen and learn."

'Uncle Charlie said he'd see you at the races, Dad. He gave me a lift from Roma.'

Dad grunted.

Baby Girl led her horse back up the paddock.

It was a rich red blood bay with black points, white socks and a blaze down to its nose. Baby Girl had her cheek resting on its neck. As the sun dappled its coat the horse gently nuzzled her. Then Baby Girl sprang up on its back and galloped away.

Mum caught her from the window. 'Tom. Tom. Quickly.'

Dad ran down the back steps. He whistled sharply and his horse, a black stallion, came trotting up from the paddock. Dad grabbed its mane then began to run with it before he leapt up on its back. He took off after her. Both rode bareback.

Baby Girl cleared the fence with a wild grin on her face. Her horse had turned one ear towards her so he could obey every command she issued, spoken or not. The other listened out for Dad. He was not far behind them. Both horses were intent on making sure their riders won. They galloped at a furious pace towards the golf course. It was mostly red sand, dusted with some surviving ancient Ooline trees and a bit of mulga. The business people were out on it swinging their clubs. Their caddies, usually an employee or their children, moved the flags.

Golfers scattered as Baby Girl and Dad pelted down the golf course. Dad was gaining on her. She kept taking quick glances over her shoulder to see how close he was. Dad was a far more experienced rider than Baby Girl but at this point in time she didn't care. She aimed her horse for the clubhouse.

Mum, still clutching her tea towel, had followed us out to the front verandah. She gasped as she clenched the tea towel into a fist.

Henry was white with fear not about what was happening now but what would happen when Dad and Baby Girl got back. The telephone lines signalled the properties around us on the party line we shared. One long, two shorts. One short, one long, three shorts. Then one by one our neighbours dribbled out of their homes to watch what was going on.

Baby Girl's horse ran up the clubhouse stairs, pounded across the verandah and charged into the main room. People ran for their lives as Dad went after her at full bore. Baby Girl flew out the back of the clubhouse and galloped down the backstretch. She cleared another fence. Dad shot over it as well. He almost had his horse alongside her. People began to cheer as Dad and Baby Girl raced neck and neck back down the main road. Baby Girl was just inches in front of Dad. The neighbours began to clap and whoop.

'She ruining my party.' Mum was in tears from fury. 'That dirty stinking little animal is ruining my party. She's doing it deliberately. I've spent months getting it together so I could have a bit of fun, but no, that filthy rotten creature has to ruin it for me.'

I began to source anything that could be used as a weapon.

Henry looked as if he was going to be sick.

Baby Girl came towards the house, took her horse over the fence and into the home paddock as Dad had originally told her to do.

I ran down the back stairs and moved quickly towards the woodheap.

Baby Girl jumped off her horse.

Dad wheeled his around, dismounted and tied it up near the water trough. Dad's horse lowered his head towards Baby Girl and her horse. Baby Girl's horse dipped his head in reply. Dad and Baby Girl took each other in, neither giving an inch.

'Git inside before I skin you alive,' was all he said.

I put the axe down.

Dad was going to let Baby Girl off instead of belting her. Sometimes he'd bash us just for looking at him the wrong way.

Dad and Baby Girl came towards the house. While Dad walked back up the stairs she sat on the steps to put the hessian bags around her feet again. Baby Girl came inside with me.

Henry was still shaking.

Dad took his chair at the head of the table. Mum topped up the teapot from the black iron kettle on the stove.

The house was a tinderbox.

'Where did you get the horse from, BG?' I decided to break the silence.

She didn't reply.

Mum poured Dad a cup of tea and handed him some Scotch Finger biscuits.

'I've said time and again, I don't want that animal anywhere near me.' Mum tried to take advantage of the situation to get her own way. 'I want you to get rid of it, Tom.'

Dad grunted.

Henry obviously couldn't stand being there for a minute longer. He and Mum exchanged covert glances as he walked past her to leave the room.

'Moody bugger.' Dad's observation was made to no one in particular.

'You.' Mum jabbed Baby Girl nun–like in the back with stiff hard fingers designed to hurt her small spine. 'I've had enough of you. Show Jennifer where she's sleeping.'

Baby Girl didn't let anyone see how much Mum'd hurt her as she got up. I picked up my swag to follow her.

Mum turned the radio on to listen to Portia Faces Life. I heard Dad scrap his chair back. He was on the run from the story "taken from the heart of every woman who had ever dared to love".

My bedroom had become Baby Girl's. I put my swag down and sat on the bed.

'You rode like the wind today, BG. You could give Gran and Greenhide a run for their money.'

Baby Girl stopped herself from looking pleased and shrugged.

'Why are you wearing bags around your feet?'

Baby Girl kept biting on the raw stumps of her fingers.

'What's going on here, BG? Why is Mum locking you out of the house?'

Baby Girl waited a long time before she replied. 'It's to keep my grimy germs and filthy dust out of her house.' She paused to chew on her fingers again. 'Mum says I'm nothing but a dirty mongrel and I take after Dad's side of the family with my giant haunches.' She finished in a rush. 'So I have to bag my feet.'

'What does Dad say about it?'

Baby Girl moved her thin shoulders.

I knew what Dad would say. "You have to look after your mother."

Finally Baby Girl looked at me. Her dark blue eyes were filled with a sadness that stretched into a faraway place that perhaps no one would ever be able to reach and even if they did, they probably wouldn't be able to bring her back from it anyway. I took her hand but after a few seconds she snatched it away from me. She too was beyond being touched except perhaps by the animals she kept around her. I'd learned to be touched from a distance by sound.

'How's Henry's Save Mum fund going?' I put my swag over near the window just in case.

'Mum says there's not enough in it so she has to stay with Dad until Henry gets some more. He's looking for another job. Now that he's better.'

'Well at least we are awake up to all his money making schemes.' I tried to think of a memory we'd shared once.

'Remember when he put a lock on the lavatory and we had to pay to get in?' I smiled at Baby Girl then pulled out my few possessions. 'Is there really going to be a birthday party? Or is it Mum just carrying on?'

'She's been organising it for months.' Baby Girl's rusty words stuck in her throat. 'She wants to show everybody.'

I patted Baby Girl's hand to tell her it was all going to be alright.

'What's the name of your horse?'

'Rebel.'

She nearly burst with pride at the name and the sentiment behind it. 'Dad got him for me.'

He'd bought some fish and chips for me and a friend I'd brought home from boarding school once. Tears welled inside me every time I thought about the kindness and generosity of his gesture. I knew he had no money to spare. He told me that all the time. It was one of the reasons I had to go out to work instead of continuing with school the way most people were.

'How about I stick around for a while? Just to keep an eye on things. As soon as I get a bit more money together I'll take you to the city with me if you want to come.'

Baby Girl'd begun to gnaw at her fingers again.

'Don't worry, BG. You can bring Rebel with you. I'll find somewhere to agist him. People still ride in the city, you know.'

On Saturday morning Mum and Henry were doing the laundry. They swirled Rekitts Bag Blue in a tub of water before they dumped the tablecloths in it. After poking the snowy white tablecloths with a stick for a few minutes Mum fed them into a mangel while Henry wound the handle around and around. Everything came out the way Mum wanted the world to be—white, and so stiffly starched with Silver Star it automatically stood to attention. Behind her back the town called her Mrs. Mangel.

When I got to the kitchen Dad was making breakfast. Mum and Henry had finished pegging the laundry needed for the party on the line and Baby Girl had fed the animals. Everyone'd gathered at the table. Dad toasted white bread over the coals with a long-handled fork he'd made out of fencing wire. When the toast was ready he turned to put it on a blue enamel plate in the middle of the table. His home churned butter, Gran's bitter native orange and lime marmalade and a jar of salty-sweet Vegemite waited to be spread on it.

Then the air changed and everyone in it became taut with tension or frozen in fear in it.

'Turn the radio on Jennifer.' Mum tried to make the request sound completely innocent. 'I'll make some more tea.'

Henry smirked.

Baby Girl hung her head and stared at her fingers then looked up at me. Be careful she warned as she glanced almost imperceptibly towards the radio. Mum began counting tealeaves a spoon at a time into the teapot from the beige canister with bright blue lettering that said *Tea* on each side.

'Go on. Turn on the radio,' Dad said. 'Git a move on.'

I walked over to the counter where the cream radio sat.

'And one for the pot,' I heard Mum say as I turned the knob to on.

A pleasant English accented male announcer was ending the news with a short broadcast by our Prime Minister, Bob Menzies. Australia was still being menaced by communism and other dark forces who had gathered enviously around us, ready to invade and steal everything we had. We had to stay vigilant to keep them out.

'I'm gittin' sick of that bloke calling workin' people like me commies. Pith and wind that bloke. Bet he'll kick the commie and union can into winnin' the next election. He'll find another Petrov to do it.'

Mum made her contribution to the conversation and politics. 'Ing,' she said.

'Ah Jennifer,' the radio announcer said over the music of Happy Birthday. 'Sweet sixteen and never been kissed, or so your mother says but we know better don't we?' Then he laughed at me. 'And here's the request for your sixteenth birthday today from all your family.'

"You come on like a dream, peaches and cream, lips like strawberry wine," Johnny Brunette began to sing.

Mum and Dad laughed in derision. Henry joined in. Baby Girl chewed on her fingertips.

Mum's laughter turned into a short snort.

'Peaches and cream. Dream on. Not with that big fat red face of yours. How you can show it in public I don't know.'

Dad got up to pour himself a rum. He downed it in one gulp then sat down again. He tapped his fingers on the table. Mum brought the teapot over. She poured Dad a cup from the old brown pot.

'It was the only song we could find that mentioned sixteen in it. None of that other guff applies to you though so don't go around big notin' yourself,' Dad said.

While Mum added an 'Ing' Baby Girl's face told me it wasn't over.

'And seein' you're sixteen it's about time you settled down.' Dad stood up to go outside again. 'You start nursin' at the hospital on Monday.'

'Ing, Tom, Ing.' Mum was beyond exasperation.

'I don't want to be a nurse.'

Dad swung on me. I stepped out of striking reach.

'Your great–grandmother Olive was a nurse, your Aunty Jane is a nurse, your Aunty Gloria was a nurse and you're gunna be a nurse.' He looked me up and down. 'And for someone as boofheaded as you are, you oughta be grateful they'll take you.'

'Besides you don't have any say in anything about what you want to do until after you turn twenty–one.' Mum had it all worked out. 'That's five years away. It's for the best. People were beginning to talk.'

My voice sounded as if it was coming from down a long thick tunnel.

'Why? I'm not doing anything wrong. I've always got work.'

'Keep your voice down.'

Mum was worried that the neighbours had crawled up to the windows to listen.

'We've had enough trouble this week.'

'You're startin' nursin' on Monday.' Dad's voice shook with a rage that was just shy of an explosion.

I checked the exits as Mum chimed in with more 'ings'.

'You can live up at the hospital too. We don't have room for you. I'm fed up to the back teeth with the lot of you—bludgers. Nothin' but trouble or worse—'. Dad looked at Henry more in sorrow than anger. 'Completely and utterly useless to a bloke.'

He walked down the back steps.

Mum turned to threaten me.

'If you don't do as you're told we're going to put you in one of those homes for uncontrollable girls. You can tell them what you will and won't do Miss Know–It–All.'

She began to clear the kitchen table.

'Well we'd better start getting the food ready for my party.'

Her voice became dreamy as she talked to herself about it.

'It's going to be a humdinger. It'll be the best birthday party I've ever had. Everybody who's anybody is going to be there—my cousin, he's now the Chairman of the Shire, and Father Forex. I'll show them. That Gloria being holier than thou about it all. And your father's mother. Telling me that we're a disgrace for not educating you just because they think you're intelligent. They obviously don't know you very well do they? Saying that the kids from The Mish are being treated better than you are because their parents are sending them to Teacher's College or putting them into the Armed Forces to learn a trade. They're only trying to show me up. Well I'll show them. They're not coming to my party. Who do they think they are? Didn't hear them offer to pay for you. Short arms and long pockets that's them. As if I would care what they think anyhow. I'm related to the Royal family. God knows what gutter your father's mob crawled out of. They were nothing but lackeys for my father and they needn't forget it. I'll show them how it's done in real society. I'll be with well–bred people who know their heritage. No one will forget my party in a hurry. I'll show them.'

Baby Girl planted her tongue in her cheek and poked it out briefly at me before she looked back down again at her fingers.

Dad came into the kitchen with an armful of wood.

Mum got out packets of Jatz crackers and some cheddar cheese. 'Henry? You can cut up the cheese.'

As Henry got up to do as he was told Mum handed me a jar of bright green gherkins.

'You can do these. Oh and Jennifer? I forgot.' Mum laughed gaily. 'Happy birthday. And you know something else? You are really going to love being at my party tonight, won't she, Tom?'

As Dad stacked the wood beside the stove he kept half an eye on Mum.

She'd begun to sing softly to herself "you're sixteen, you're beautiful and you're mine" as she iced the birthday cake.

THE PARTY

The last birthday party I'd had was in first grade. I'd invited all the kids over from The Mish and in my class. We'd had a whale of a time. The trouble was most of my guests hadn't told their parents where they were and a manhunt was on by the time they started to go home.

For my sixteenth birthday party, I wore a dress my city cousin had given me because it was too out of date for her. She'd smoothed down the skirt as I modeled it for her. "It takes ten years or more for anything to change out there so don't worry. It'll still be fashionable." It was candy striped and had ruffled rope petticoats underneath it. Baby Girl wore a white shirt and fawn riding jodhpurs. She'd Brylcreemed her hair so it lay flat on her head. Her outfit was completed with brown elastic sided boots. I was determined to make the party something to remember.

'We'll make it lots of fun, BG. We'll dance and sing.' I got carried away. 'Maybe we can invite people home after it. It'd be wonderful to fill the house full of people, laughing and talking, playing some music, wouldn't it?'

Baby Girl used her tongue to poke her false teeth out at me. They now hung over her bottom lip grinning at me. Her original teeth had been kicked out by a horse a few years ago. Her feet had slipped through the stirrup irons and she'd fallen over the rump then underneath its back legs. He'd kicked her across her face so all she lost were her top teeth. If he'd kicked upwards she would've been dead. Maybe she was right but it would've been nice to have some friends to talk to.

'Put those teeth away,' I said.

With a last glance in the mirror and another to anxiously check the back of my dress we walked into the lounge room.

Henry and Dad were dressed casually as well.

You should change.

For once Mum didn't say a word about how we looked.

You've got the wrong clothes on.

When we arrived at the CWA Hall everyone else was wearing sleek sheath skirts, slender tops and high heels. Mum looked at me and laughed. She too was dressed in a tight black sheath skirt with a black top. It stopped at chest level before it became attached to pale pink silk that was scalloped around what she called her décolletage. Her black patent leather stilettoes made her long legs look longer.

I looked like Dali's chuppa-chup wrapper.

While Baby Girl went with Dad and Henry to help with the food, I found a corner. Around me girls were examining the labels on each other's clothes. Dress labels defined not only how much money you had but also what social group you belonged in or would by the time they'd finished with you. Some had given me presents—a crystal cut perfume bottle and a matching bell, a tiny brown horse figurine, a few deers and some soap.

Rock 'n roll blared from tinny speakers. I slowly recalled the names of everyone at the party but I didn't know who they were. They'd stayed in the town and would, no doubt, form eventual marriages out of life–long friendships. No one could really remember me. From the years of being in convents with several hundred girls crammed into a room for the thirty minutes of recreation time we were granted I realised I didn't know how to talk. I had no education and now I didn't know how to conduct a conversation. I had nothing to say anyway. The more crowded the room became the lonelier and more isolated I felt in it. I was stuck in silence. This was followed by shame. Stupid came soon after that.

I'd read every library book I could, sometimes seven or more a week, but none of them told me how to fit in unless of course, I was in Russia with Dostoyevsky or Tolstoy and a revolution was in full swing. I was pig ignorant. The only template I had for a relationship was my parents and the family. They resembled four or five rounds with Sharman's boxers rather than a love song. I tried to listen to the others easy banter and smiled but not too much. I hoped I looked as if I knew what they were talking about but it was evident I'd been left behind a long time ago. Old age began to creep through my bones again while at the same time I felt so immature I thought I'd never be able to grow up.

I went down the veranda and sat on the top step of the stairs. From there I could see the campfires at The Mish and two or three lights twinkling in the town. It was slowly getting electricity but the nightsoil man was still driving down the street to empty the pans from the outside lavatories. I tried to cheer myself up by humming along to a song the band inside was playing when I became aware that someone was standing behind me. Quickly I turned to see who it was. He was short with dark curly hair. He was dressed like a jackaroo in moleskins, a checked shirt and riding boots. I began to panic. My brain froze.

He smiled at me then indicated he wanted to go past. I wondered if I should run back inside rather than be alone with a stranger but by the time I went to make a move, he was already going past me. I tried to calm myself down by looking at the campfires and humming to the music. He walked down a few steps then he turned around and still smiling he smashed his fist into my face.

I tumbled over and over all the way down the steps and sprawled in the dirt. He walked down and stood over me. I half picked myself up from the dirt, stunned and unable to cry or call out.

'That'll teach you to think you're better than me.'

He had a soft Scottish burr. He put his riding boot on the back of my neck to force me down into the dirt again and rolled it so he could rub my face in it.

'Stuck up bitch.'

With a final push on my neck he took his foot away and disappeared into the darkness.

'You must've done something.' Henry had found me as I staggered back up the stairs. 'He's a really nice guy.'

'You must've done something.' One of Henry's friends was having a cigarette on the verandah. 'He'd never do anything like that to anyone for no reason.'

'You must've done somethink to provoke him. People don't do somethink like that about nothin'. You're just going to have to learn to behave yourself.' Dad stopped before he added, 'Talk about a flamin' boofhead. You take the cake.'

Baby Girl came to stand beside me.

'Trust you to ruin my party.' Mum was beyond fury as she tried to salvage the night. 'Go home and stop your boy crazy nonsense. Go on, get. Take Belinda with you. You're the lowest of the low.'

In the morning I tried to cover the bruise with make–up.

As I trudged down the road towards the hospital I decided I had to make my life work out for me by myself. I wasn't going to get any help from anyone. Besides, it was too dangerous to ask for help even if I knew how. Maybe they were right. Maybe it was my fault for being alone with someone I'd never seen before even though I hadn't meant to. I hadn't been able to read his mind even though I should've been able to. It was clear I couldn't live in the town for very long. I was a trouble–maker and I couldn't be trusted.

All I had going for me it seemed a few pounds in my pocket, some advice from Uncle Lincoln, an ability to play the piano, read books and practice poverty, chastity, and obedience, and do it all in silence or was I just silenced. Maybe that's why on some occasions I could speak and on others not a single sound comes out. I could always think of what I could have said or done weeks or months later. It was always witty and wise. Sometimes my words'd cut people down to size, other times, I was heroically triumphant over a spluttering enemy.

I blew on a stem of thistledown to make a wish that everything'd turn out alright. I crossed the fingers on my right hand for good luck. Between the road behind me and the hospital up on the hill I set my face into a blank mask so nobody could read anything into it or know what was going on inside. I'd have to stay like that until I got some brains, grew up more or better still make enough money to get Baby Girl and me away from here.

I had nothing to lose by working at the hospital for a while—except perhaps life itself but then that'd always been on the cards. Dying didn't scare me. It was a wonder the nuns hadn't killed me already with beatings and castor oil.

I didn't have the education I needed to make something of myself. I knew nothing about relationships. I didn't know how to talk to people. The only love I knew about was from my fleeting moments with the blackfellas at The Mish and Aunty Bloss. My knowledge of what love was I culled from the odd movie or book. Being uglier than sin I knew I could never be like the women I saw on the screen. I had little money and no home. I had no mob to belong to and according to Mum I hadn't even made it out of the gutter yet so I wasn't even at life's starting line.

Once I got to it I'd give it a go; see what happened; even though my bones creaked and ached and hurt from being so old.

Life couldn't get any worse, I told myself.

Really.

It couldn't.

PIG

The rifle shot ricocheted through the air. The pig screamed then silence fell for a few seconds. Words and the odd laugh from the cattle yards drifted towards us as Dad and Uncle Rhodie hung the kill to blood it.

Mum drew heavily on a cigarette. Her hand shook. Henry'd brought her a cup of tea. He sat opposite her, ashen faced.

'I can't stand it much longer. I just can't stand it. I want you to go on Sunday.' Mum was beyond desperation. 'You can take the train to the city.'

Henry shuffled in the kitchen chair.

'I don't like to leave you alone with him.'

He was growing out of his old jeans and t–shirt. He never bought anything new. Every penny he earned was hoarded to help Mum leave Dad.

'Well you can't stay here. The sooner you go the better it will be for everyone.' Mum had her reasons for leaving town as soon as she could. 'I want to get my food from a supermarket not some amateur abattoir in the back yard.'

Mum was dressed in navy blue slacks. Tucked into it was a black peasant blouse with a scooped neck and short puff sleeves. Red and green flowers danced in decoration around the neckline. A black patent leather belt, black stilettos and a big green bracelet completed the outfit. They'd forgotten I was there.

'I should have enough shortly.'

Henry revelled in his saving her role.

'Well, we'll see how you go.' Mum gave a short but tragic toss of her head. Her hair was immaculately coiffured and stiffened with hair spray.

I decided to add my two cents worth to the conversation.

'Why don't you go to the city with him, Mum? Dad and I can look after BG.'

Mum looked slightly startled as if she had only just realised I'd heard them.

'You could get a job there and live the way you want to. You don't have to stay here.'

Mum spat venom at me.

'Your father told me if I married him I'd never have to work again.'

Henry too was furious.

'Why don't you mind your own business? We didn't ask you to butt in.'

I shrugged.

'Mum worked in a shop before. She could work in one again. Maybe she could get a job with her brother. He's got a shop near the city.'

Dad came in with half a pig carcass on his shoulder.

'Just bringin' home the bacon.'

His smile sparkled into his bright blue eyes then turned into a quiet pride about his skills as a bushman. As I laughed at his joke tears sprang into my eyes. I always ended up in tears when I meant to laugh.

'Ing!' Mum shook from rage. 'Ing!'

She stormed towards the lounge room. Her stilettos clicked on the linoleum, pitting it as she went. The lid of the piano banged up and Mum began to thump out some Chopin. The doctor had told her to play the piano every day to exercise the arm she had cut with a scythe a few years before. But she mainly used the piano to stop the neighbours from hearing Dad belt us.

Every Saturday afternoon Dad'd merrily come home from the pub, have a few words with Mum then had a short sleep that made him cranky when he woke up. Afterwards we'd be lined up outside the bathroom for our beating. Dad took us in one by one. Henry went first, fitting and falling in terror through the doorway.

Mum thumped out Side-by-Side, Blue Skies, Dear Hearts and Gentle People and How Much Is That Doggie in the Window to cover any noise.

As I heard Henry scream with each slash of the razor strop I was torn this way and that, between running away or trying to rescue him, knowing if I did anything I'd make things worse.

I'd tried to beat Dad away with a mop once but that only made him hit us more. Because she was still little Baby Girl only got a small amount of the strop. She remained silent throughout. I did too. But nothing would've come out of my mouth anyway. I knew better. We'd come out of the bathroom bewildered and broken—our beaten bodies rigid with fear and desperation. We'd sit out on the back steps with our faces turned away from one another until the sadness and shame reached the end of our limbs and numbed us with pins and needles. We looked like gargoyles eternally guarding a ruined temple.

After that it was Mum's turn to assault us with hot soap and water then we'd start our chores. Later we'd go to the pictures. We never knew why Dad beat us. Sometimes he used to tell us stories that were so funny and fantastical we never wanted to leave his side. Other times, despite our best efforts to please him and to be good, it was never enough. "Just whippin' you into shape," he used to quip. "Hurts me more than it hurts you."

All week at school we were thrashed by the nuns. Henry's left arm was bruised, swollen and useless. My back to my knees was frozen into a permanent spasm. Baby Girl denied her girlishness to be the kind of boy the nuns liked, provided they were right-handed.

Dad had put the pig carcass down on the kitchen bench.

'What's wrong with her?'

'I'm going to the city on Sunday.'

Henry was obviously expecting Dad to kick up a stink about it.

'There's a credit squeeze on thanks to Menzies latest attempt to manage the joint. There's not much work around. You'll probably pick up something though. Your uncle Harry'll help.'

Dad gave a loud whistle. Baby Girl materialised from the shadows. She got out the carving utensils and dutifully handed them to Dad, handle first. He expertly butchered the pig.

'He'd go broke running a brewery that bloke.' Dad grunted as he made his final comment on the Prime Minister and his government. 'Too busy drinkin' all the profits.'

While they were engrossed in splitting the pig up I slipped away to go back up to the hospital.

Gran had been admitted a week or so ago with stomach pains. She'd been sucking on Rennie's indigestion tablets for several years but the pain had grown worse. Grandfather wouldn't pay for a private room but I'd managed to manoeuvre her into a corner in the women's ward where, with one flick of the white curtains, she had privacy.

Bronwyn, a nursing sister with a triangular nun-like white veil on her head was force–feeding Gran. She shovelled the food into Gran's mouth not waiting for her to swallow. The mush ran down Gran's chin and onto a bib placed roughly over her pale pink nightdress. She moaned in distress.

'For God's sake.' Bronwyn was determined to empty the dish into Gran's mouth even if she couldn't eat it just to tick it off her list of chores.

Her mother was a reluctant seamstress who'd been abandoned by her husband many years before. They'd lived in a slab hut over near the water tower. There was little in the way of government help or social security for deserted women. Her Catholic husband never paid for the eight children he'd left behind by the time she was thirty but then most men didn't. If their wives hadn't said, done or been the wrong thing, the men'd never have left them in the first place, they said. Men seemed to spend a lot of time making up the sort of woman they wanted but after she failed to meet his specifications she ended up being ditched while the men set out to design a better one.

Abandoned women lived from hand to mouth. Other women and society shunned them. As soon as their husbands'd shot through their mates'd come around immediately to see if their former friend's wife needed any help. "Not the sort they were offering," Dad'd snort.

The police'd track the men down from town to town but they'd move on as quickly as they were found, usually leaving even more children behind.

"Those Catholics seem to treat women like milking cows, only good for reproducing to provide more Catholics. Barely had one when they're having another," Uncle Lincoln'd said some time back when I went over to visit him. "I don't see the Pope paying for all those kiddies when those blokes shoot through. You'd think he'd sell something to raise money to help them out instead of trying to get more out of them on Sundays. The women are hard pressed to feed anyone let alone themselves. We followed the lead of the kangaroo. Best mothers in the world, 'roos. Like them, we only have kids when the circumstances suit. Our mob, we don't ever give up working either. You never know when you'll need the moolah. You always gotta make sure you've got work."

Bronwyn's resentment about her family situation was taken out on the defenceless in her care, particularly the elderly and babies.

I snatched the spoon from her. 'I'll do it.'

'I don't know why we bother feeding her. It's a waste of time. She can't digest it. She's riddled with cancer.'

As Bronwyn walked away I pulled the curtains around Gran to shield her from seeing her husband coming up the stairs with a giant bouquet of fresh flowers. He'd spruced himself up and was dressed to the nines. He knocked on the Matron's door.

'It's alright, Gran, she's gone.'

I put the spoon down and picked up her washer. I gently cleaned her face. Gran put her withered hand on mine—even the gentlest touch made her skin hurt.

I sat near her pillows and cradled her in my arms. Her blue eyes and long dark lashes were so large they took up most of her face. I touched the hands that had cooked thousands of meals, did her best for nearly thirty children, most of whom weren't hers, midwifed some more, made vats of soap with lime and lard and rode horses like the wind while she scattered wildflowers to walk in when it rained. She looked as if she'd come to the end of what a hard life had thrown at her. She was begging not to be hurt by anything or anybody anymore. I stroked her hair. I didn't know how to take her pain away.

'Where's Father?' She managed to say.

I slid off the bed. 'I'll get him.'

Her black curly hair fell starkly against the white bed linen that encased her like a shroud. I put her favourite tortoiseshell clips in on either side of her hair to hold it away from her face.

'I'll be back in a minute or so.'

The Matron came out of her office. She was in her early thirties. Her friends had come with her to help run the hospital. They were all on the lookout for a rich grazier Mum'd told me.

It seemed Grandfather was presenting himself as a suitable candidate.

I couldn't hear what he was saying but the Matron was obviously buttering him up as she accepted the flowers. She smelled them, was overcome with delight and put her hand on his chest.

Out of nowhere Aunty Gloria pounced. She snatched the flowers from the Matron.

'Flowers!' she exclaimed. 'For your wife.' Her bright brown button eyes bored into Grandfather's. 'Let's take them to her at once. She'll love them won't she—Grandfather?'

After she gave me a filthy look the Matron retreated to her office.

Aunty Gloria turned on Grandfather. She was only half his size but her temper made her look bigger.

'You rotten old mongrel. You could've waited. God knows Goody waited on you hand and foot for over fifty years. A few more weeks wouldn't kill you.'

Grandfather grunted then made his way to Gran's ward while we stopped at the kitchen.

Rosemary, Beulah's Mum from The Mish got out a vase and filled it with warm bore water.

'Saw froggy was a-courtin'. There's no accounting for some blokes. He wouldn't have a penny if it weren't for her working her guts out.'

'Don't get me started Rosemary. Goody adores that old coot.'

Aunty Gloria bustled around the kitchen to find some scissors then took the ends off the stems before she arranged the flowers beautifully in the vase. 'Your Gran will be very happy to get these. She always loved flowers.'

Grandfather was waiting outside the ward.

Aunty Gloria thrust the vase in his hands. 'You get in there and behave yourself. Shame on you.'

With bright smiles on our faces we walked up to Gran's bed with Grandfather.

He gracelessly dumped the vase of flowers on the side table. 'Got them from the city. They flew in on the plane this morning.'

Gran put her trembling paper–thin hand out to him. He briefly held it before dropping it to the sheet. He picked it up again when he saw the murderous look on Aunty Gloria's face. She was determined he was going to be the kind of husband Gran had always wanted even if it wasn't true.

I held the flowers near Gran's face so she could smell them.

We chatted to her until she began to drift off to sleep. We kissed her on her withered cheek and told her we'd see her in the morning.

Grandfather left to pick up some stale bread from the bakery to feed the dogs. They only got meat when it was time to muster.

'Do you want to come home for lunch?' Aunty Gloria asked me as we walked down the hospital verandah. She always moved at a half–trot half–run with a nervous quickness about her. 'I've hardly had a minute to myself let alone sit down to talk to you and ask you how you are.'

Her kids were playing under a sprinkler on the back lawn as we drove in. Mrs. Feeney, their next–door neighbours was still in her cage on the front verandah. Her husband had put her in it to keep her off Bex powders. He could keep an eye on her from the small shop he worked in across the road. With a pot of tea on a tray and cigarettes she was well set up with some books piled up on a small table within easy reach of her hand. She flicked through the Woman's Weekly as she listened to cowboy music from the radio. She waved unsteadily as we went past.

'She's still getting the Bex,' Aunty Gloria told me in a grim tone. 'Nothing stops those sorts of people. Nothing.'

She turned the hose off on her way through to the kitchen.

'Time to clean up for lunch,' she announced cheerily to the children. She bustled up the back stairs.

'Rhodie should've finished dressing the pig by now. We'll have some nice pork chops. I'll dust them with some mustard powder to cheer them up a bit.'

Aunty Gloria flew around the kitchen, in and out of cupboards, and over the stove. It seemed within minutes she had filled the table with baked potatoes, pumpkin, carrots and pork chops. Watermelon jelly and custard made Uncle Rhodie smile. I liked his smile. It slipped up the side of his face and his gold tooth gleamed.

After lunch we sat in the small green parlour with the bone china ducks flying in formation up the wall. Aunty Gloria loved ornaments. They were crammed into every bit of spare space throughout the house. Her kids had the job of dusting them. If looks could kill then every duck and shepherd'd be dead within seconds.

Uncle Rhodie'd taken the kids up to the Irish Giant's betting shop at the back of the pub. He called it walking the dog or going to see his wheelchair–bound brother, Uncle Darcy. I don't know why he bothered to try to fool Aunty Gloria. She knew exactly where he was at all times and what he was up to.

"She's got eyes in the back of her head that Gloria," Dad'd observed once. "Need to have them where Rhodie's concerned."

Uncle Rhodie'd been thrown out the back of a ute as it sped down a jump–up and overturned. He'd landed on his head. After a long life and death struggle in hospital both in the town and in the city, Uncle

Rhodie'd survived but he had no short–term memory, especially when he bent over. "His skull pressed onto his brain," Mum'd said.

Grandfather took full advantage of it. He gave Rhodie a job "to help him out". Grandfather used to assure Rhodie that he'd paid him his weekly wage but Rhodie could never remember getting it or what he had done with it if he had got it.

Aunty Gloria soon put a stop to Grandfather's shenanigans. She became a shearer's cook. She took Rhodie and her kids on the road cooking from shearing shed to shearing shed. Today she was back in her little green and white timber house preparing the next contract.

'Now.' We'd settled into the brown tapestry armchairs and Aunty Gloria was pouring tea. 'What we need to do is find you a decent husband.'

It took me a while to get my breath.

'I don't want to get married.' I added emphatically in case she didn't understand what I was saying. 'Ever.'

I'd been going to marry Mattie when I was a little but after his father died from the grog they'd moved on to a city down south where his mother could get some work. I'd probably never see him again. After watching Mum and Dad's marriage and my relatives' I couldn't see what good it did anyone.

The Mad Goat Lady had sorted out God, religion and marriage for me years ago. She'd said that according to the church, God created a man and a woman in original sin. Then God got a woman pregnant with himself so he could be born on earth. Once God was born he decided to sacrifice himself as a sacrifice to himself to save everyone from the sin he'd given them in the first place. "There's one born every minute." The Mad Goat Lady used to say as she howled with laughter. "What a load of hooey."

The only other marriages I knew about were the one the nuns and priests had. Hundreds of thousands of nuns married the same man, God without anyone calling him a pants man. The priests couldn't marry anyone, real or imagined. While God got married millions of times his subjects could only marry once. They were never allowed to get a divorce no matter what. There was only one woman on earth that men allowed to get away with her story that God had made her pregnant to explain a child born on the wrong side of the blanket. Every other woman was a liar who needed to be controlled by men and the law in order to keep her in line.

One of the girls I'd gone to school with had presented at the hospital with severe stomach pains. Her mother was very distressed and the girl didn't want anyone to touch her. When she finally got undressed the staff discovered she had bound her body so tightly with a corset that it had grown into her body. When the corset was cut off her child was born and whisked away without asking her permission, never to be heard of again.

"No one will ever marry her," Mum'd declared, and besides she had let the world know exactly what type of girl she was by chewing gum. Only Americans chewed gum.

I preferred Uncle Lincoln's marriage method. He'd made a decent fire so his future wife could warm herself up by it. Then he made her some tucker and invited her to sit beside him to eat.

Aunty Gloria smiled. 'Now, now. I've got someone very special in mind. He's a jackaroo out on the Companoni place. He's well educated and his parents are quite wealthy. He's very keen to meet you.'

Years ago I'd been out on there with Dad. Mr. Companoni lived in the main homestead; alongside it was another house for his manager and his family. Next he'd built rows of homes on either side of the main house for all the blackfellas who'd grown too old to work so they could still fossick around the place. His family and the manager's wife devoted themselves to looking after them and their families. "Never met anyone who made so many pickles and jams as that manager's wife," Dad noted. "It hardly gets a chance to grow into anythink before it gets preserved or jarred."

There'd been a big fire out there too. Dad'd given us wet hessian bags to thump on it. After we thought we had it out Dad saw it roaring towards the house. He threw us in the bathtub and lay over the top of us. His back blistered from the heat. Later we surveyed the blackened earth. All the chooks were dead in their pens. The dogs'd died on their chains. The fire had hidden inside a tree and, when it was ready, it crashed across the old corrugated road to torch the other side.

I tried to fob off Aunty Gloria's suggestion but to my horror I began to cry. I'd forgotten it happened when I laughed more than twice at any one time. I'd always tried to avoid laughter. I also cried if someone was kind to me. I shrank from it too. The tears soon turned into sobs and, even though I dug my fingernails into my arms to draw blood, I couldn't stop.

'What on earth's the matter?' Aunty Gloria sounded perplexed and anxious. 'I am so sorry. I didn't realise it would upset you.' She cupped my face in her hands. 'They're not all like the idiot at your party. Those kind of men hit women because they can not because you did anything wrong. Come on. Don't cry.'

Her kindness made it worse. I tried to stop.

'I can't be seen in public.' I tried desperately to pull myself together. 'Mum says—.'

Aunty Gloria pursed her lips. 'You shouldn't take any notice of what Rene has to say about you. Or anybody for that matter. There's nothing wrong with the way you look. I think you look quite pretty.' Aunty Gloria paused trying to search for the right words. 'Rene thinks of herself as a lily on a dustbin—a gilded lily at that. She should never've married Tom. He should never've married her. Tom really should've bought that racehorse he always talks about or married Bessie Balfour. Still he should get the guts to stick Rene back in her box when she starts up instead of thinking all mothers are like your grandmother and have to be worshipped. He put her up on a pedestal and now he doesn't know how to get her off it. Still it's no reason for Rene to take it out on you or poor little BG for that matter.'

'Henry's leaving on Sunday. He's going to get more money together so she can leave Dad and go to the city to live.' My words came out in gulps.

'Sending a boy out to do her job for her is she?' Aunty Gloria turned to me. 'All the more reason you should meet this young fella I've found. I've organised for him to take you to the pictures next Saturday.'

Tim turned up on the front verandah of the hospital with a box of chocolates in his hand. He'd had them flown in from the city. We never had chocolates because the desert heat turned them into mud within minutes. We treated ourselves occasionally to raspberry jellies, bullseyes and boiled humbugs because nothing'd melt them. I'd put on the only other dress I possessed. It was green, blue, and black striped and slightly off the shoulder. Mum'd told me I looked like a circus tent when I'd brought it home to show her but it was all I could afford.

I'd tried to memorise what Tim looked like but he was a blur. He'd opened the car door for me. I'd tried not to look like a tent or anything else so I folded my dress across my knees and held it tight while I got in the car. My hand stayed on the door handle just in case. Tim drove up to the picture theatre and parked. Aunty Gloria and Uncle Rhodie were waiting for us. My mouth wouldn't work. Everything was dizzy. I couldn't get my breath. My heart was pounding. We walked into the theatre and sat down. The lights dimmed to start the newsreel.

I knew I had to handle the box of chocolates quickly and in a ladylike manner. The cellophane wouldn't come off. It was wrapped so tightly it took forever to peel away. Finally the lid came loose and the contents rattled loudly in the box. They were still in one piece. I waited until they settled down before I offered them to Tim. He took a chocolate as did Aunty Gloria and Uncle Rhodie. I waited unsure whether I should have one or not. I had lipstick on. I didn't know whether I was supposed to eat. I felt sick and breathless. I didn't know what to do.

Aunty Gloria nudged me. I took it as the hint to have a chocolate. As I put my hand in the box it sank into a wet dark melted morass. I wasn't game to take it out. Halfway through the first movie Tim went to hold my hand but I kept it in the box. When the lights came on at interval I looked at my dark brown chocolaty mitt and bolted from the theatre. I kept my hand in the box until I made it to a darkened street where I flicked it off. I sneaked into the hospital's bathroom to wash my hands. I vowed I'd never go on a date again. Or eat chocolate. Aunty Gloria saw me a few days later when she was visiting Gran. She wasn't deterred.

'You should've just laughed it off. I guess you're still at that awkward stage. Not to worry. Plenty more fish in the sea.'

I had no interest in fish or anything else. I was saving all my money to go to the city to write and play piano. And if Henry's plans didn't work, and Mum was still with Dad, Baby Girl and her horse would have to come with me.

The Matron had decided that, after her confrontation with Aunty Gloria over Gran's flowers, to make my life misery. Every time I got to sleep the night staff would come around to shine a torch in my face. The Matron said it was part of her duty of care to make sure all the nurses were in bed alone and not out running wild in the town. After my shift finished she'd make me report back to work. The staff would pull all the hospital linen down from the shelves then order me to re–fold it, and place it back up, then they'd pull it down again.

The Mad Goat Lady was a patient in the women's ward. 'Women will never get anywhere as long as they attack each other. It suits men to keep you at each other's throats,' she told them.

Her go at the Matron only made things worse.

My shifts stretched into nearly twenty–four hours a day. When the night shift finished we had to sit in the dining room to wait for lectures from the doctor. He never gave any but we couldn't leave to go to sleep until we were dismissed by either him or the Matron. We had to stand when staff more senior to us entered a room. If they didn't tell us to sit then we had to keep standing. We seldom ate. I had become foggy from lack of sleep and thin from lack of food. I knew from boarding school I could always fill up on water but it was a short–term solution.

One night after I went to bed Julie another trainee nurse shook me awake. Julie had white blonde hair, a dark tan, giant green eyes and a cheeky attitude. Mum didn't want me to have anything to do with her because her father had been a shearer like Dad but he'd won a block of land in a Government ballot and become part of the landed gentry. Julie was keen on a grazier's son but Mum said there was no way his family would allow their son to marry the likes of Julie. He was made for better things and Julie was nothing more than mutton dressed up as lamb or something. I felt ashamed every time I looked at Julie and she smiled at me. The Matron and her friends disliked Julie as much as they did me. Perhaps it was because the patients warmed to her but I suspected it was because she was prettier than they could ever hope to be.

Julie put her fingers to her lips and whispered to get dressed. I moved out of the staff quarters silently with her. She told me the night staff was going to cover for us.

'We're going to have the best time. We're going to have ourselves a party to end all parties,' she said.

As I followed her out I thought of all the parties I'd seen at the movies or read about. Would it be a viva Las Vegas resort style or a Jay Gatsby elegant extravaganza? If anyone knew how to throw a party it would be Julie. I was thrilled she asked me to go with her.

I mentally consulted the list of what I was allowed to use during small talk. One never mentioned politics, religion or going to the lavatory for instance. Mum was so horrified by one girl she'd cut the entire family out of our lives. Their daughter had announced she had to go to the lavatory before she went out. Ladies never went to the lavatory much less spoke about the need to use it.

"She was so ill–bred she'd shortened the word to lav. Lav!" Mum'd fumed about it for weeks. "That told me all I needed to know about those kind of people."

She'd added that one only used the word napkin not serviette or any other Frenchified words that only displayed one's ignorance and lower class upbringing. You either used the proper French words for something or you used the British. Neither did one tell one anything about anything that was happening in one's family or extended family. And one always used one when talking about one.

Out in the car park a bunch of other hospital employees were already sitting in an old red utility. Julie climbed in the back of the ute and gestured for me to follow. As I did Goose Ganders, the driver, let the ute roll away from the hospital and down the hill before he turned the engine on. I noticed a lot of rifles along with Hammerhead, Lofty, Puddin' and Bluey—boys I'd gone to school with years ago.

In hushed tones Julie told me where we were going. 'It's a huntin' party. Kangaroos.'

My heart sank. I'd been on 'roo shoots with Uncle Darcy. He used to be so sloshed he couldn't tell the difference between us or the 'roos. His dogs were tied to the front of his wheelchair so it became a sled. They'd pulled him along at breakneck speed while he fired at anything that moved and we ran for our lives.

Kangaroos were the most beautiful creatures—fine strong cheekbones and gigantic soft brown eyes. Baby Girl used to milk the mothers for the joeys she'd found in the pouches of their dead mothers. I didn't want to kill them. I wanted to sing and dance and have witty conversation with intelligent people.

Everyone in the ute was drinking beer. They passed the bottle along to me.

'No thanks. I don't drink.'

Aunty Gloria never touched the grog either. Both her parents were violent alcoholics. When they weren't bashing each other they were bashing their children senseless.

"I was only little." Aunty Gloria used to tell me. "I was a tiny, tiny child. How could they?"

In some ways I envied someone who was on the turps. When I got up in the morning I knew that was how I was going to be for the rest of the day. When Dad and all the other relatives got out of bed they could turn the day into whatever they wanted with a bit of grog. By nightfall they were usually at the mercy of whatever came their way but they seemed to have a good time up to that point.

The others in the ute began to chiack me by asking me what kind of man I thought I was that I didn't join in with them. Eventually Julie told them to leave me alone but I was already on high alert.

The full moon shone through the oolong trees. The wildlife began to move. Goose turned his spotlight on. It lit up a 'roo. The chase began. Everyone'd begun to bang on the sides of the ute to scare the 'roo even more. Rifle shots peppered in and around it. The doe took a bullet to her shoulder. She threw a small terrified joey out of her pouch in a desperate attempt to save it. The ute slowed down. Julie and some others jumped out. The moonlight and the spotlight flickered in and around the bush. It was hard to hide. Julie started to run the joey down. Some of the boys began shooting wildly at trees. Bark flew off. One shot the doe through the chest as she tried to get away. She fell. The boys were whooping and shouting. The ute braked. Goose ran off with the boys to try to kill anything that moved.

The doe tried to prop herself up to see where her joey was. Julie had caught up to it. In the glare of the spotlight she began to club it with the butt of her rifle. I ran over to the doe. Although it was mortally wounded she still tried to get to her baby. It was crying out to her. She was calling it. Julie threw the rifle down and began to stomp on the joey's head. It seemed she had gone crazy trying to kill it. As the moonlight flickered on her Julie jumped up and down as blood and intestines spurted out. The boys, hooting and hollering egged her on. Dust formed a thin red mist.

The doe looked at me. I tried to block her view. She put her paw out to me. As I knelt beside her I took it and cradled her head in my arms. Her big brown liquid eyes begged me not to harm her. I stroked her as I saw out of the corner of my eye that Julie had picked up the rifle again and was bashing the butt into the joey.

After they had exhausted themselves everyone got back into the ute. I could hear them call me but I stayed with the 'roo until she died. I went over to her joey and brought it back. I placed it on top of its mother. I broke some gum tree branches off to cover them up.

As I walked away other 'roos came out of hiding and hopped over to them. They stood around in a semi–circle and watched me leave. Their mourning songs hummed through the bush as I made my way back out to the red dirt gravel road to walk into town.

The bottles of water the swagmen had planted for their kids allowed me to rinse the taste of blood and dust from my throat. As the big white moon faded a misty smoke swirled around the stars. They were massed in their millions across the sky. As I stopped to watch them I disappeared into a speck of their dust.

It was still dark when I tapped on Baby Girl's window. Silently she helped me in and we got into bed. Eventually we dozed off.

Around dawn I woke to find Gran standing by the bed. She was dressed in her best dark blue and pale pink floral dress. Her dark curly hair fell down to her shoulders. Her lips were red and her cheeks were flushed. She looked as if she was only seventeen, brightly blue–eyed, ready and eager to begin her life. She bent to kiss me before she kissed Baby Girl. Baby Girl took my hand as we watched Gran faded away.

I waited for a few minutes to make up my mind.

'I'll have to go soon, BG. Don't worry. I'll come back for you. I need to get away from Mum and Dad and find a place for us to stay. For that I need money. Lots of it. If anything goes wrong and Aunty Gloria isn't around go over to The Mish. Uncle Lincoln will help you.'

Baby Girl let my hand go and rolled on her side away from me.

As I tried to leave the house as quietly as I could Mum made her way to the telephone.

She was dressed in the heavily embroidered rose gold kimono her brother had bought back from Japan after the war. Her feet were shod in dark green quilted velvet slippers with a high heel. She looked a little surprised to see me.

I was still in dusty bloodstained clothes.

'I was just going to ring the hospital to find out how your Grandmother is.'

'She died a few minutes ago.'

33

Mum stopped then slightly glowing her green eyes filled with compassion and a touch of sadness. She turned into a woman I'd never seen before. She held her hand out to me.

'How about we sit down over breakfast and talk?'

In an achingly beautiful voice she beckoned me to join her and never leave.

'I think it's time we got to know each other, don't you? You know, Jennifer I never wanted you to leave home. I've been worried sick about you ever since.'

I was lost for words and possessed by terror.

'You're too late.'

I ran up the road to the hospital to help prepare Gran for her funeral.

THE JOKE

A large black, grey and navy blue knot had gathered outside the Church of England. Gran's boys, both black, brown and white, shouldered her coffin up the stairs into the Church.

Several hundred townspeople of all kin and colours followed.

Uncle Lincoln led his mob in from The Mish: sorry business. They all held small branches broken from various trees as much for ceremony as to swat flies. They sat down in and around the rest of the family.

Mum was dressed in black with a shiny black hat that had a large ornamental red rose on its side. Black spotted netting formed a veil over half her face. Dad wore his navy blue wedding suit. Uncle Rhodie's was grey.

Aunty Gloria too was dressed in black. "The children kept quiet for once," she said later as she rushed around the kitchen to prepare food for the wake.

Some relatives couldn't make it.

Dad's sister-in-law Aunty Audrey sent her regrets saying Uncle Joe was not feeling well. He'd been on a bender ever since Gran died. The doctor'd told him to quit drinking or else he'd be dead within six months. Uncle Joe'd bet the doctor a thousand pounds he'd last twelve. They shook on it. Aunty Audrey'd always serve up his dinner and put it on the empty spot at the table for him. "He is a very good provider," she told her only child, Max. "So I provide for him." Uncle Joe was never home very much to eat anything. He preferred to spend every spare second drinking with his mates at the pub.

Aunty Iris' husband Uncle Sly'd telephoned Dad to tell him that Iris had taken to cleaning ever since she heard about her mother's death.

She'd scrubbed the enamel from the gas stove and was currently on the roof with a tub of Gumption, a bucket of water and a nailbrush. She wanted any planes going overhead to see its sparkling roof and know she kept a beautifully clean home. The city was in the middle of a storm that had been raging for days and they were having difficulty getting her down. I'd stayed with her once. At three thirty in the morning, she'd entered the bedroom, striped the bed, stripped me and took everything to the laundry. She always did the washing and the ironing before she went to work. Everything including my pyjamas was starched. Our family liked cleaning.

Flushed in the face Henry ran in. He'd got a lift back home with Uncle Harry. They'd driven all night from the city. Henry put a small bag down on the floor, genuflected and then sat in the pew near Baby Girl and me. Looking very pleased with himself he gave Mum a small wave. She didn't return it. Instead she fixed her gaze on a holy picture nailed up on the back wall. Henry looked a bit crestfallen.

Uncle Harry took his place alongside Grandfather. He didn't bother with ceremony. Most of church had declared themselves atheists long ago but they were making half–hearted efforts to keep up with the priest.

Aunty Doll sat alongside Grandfather and Greenhide. Aunty Doll was distraught. Her son, Freddie, the communist sat with them. Doll'd had Freddie by Grandfather's brother before she'd married her current husband. Gran and Grandfather had adopted Freddie and he was now officially Dad's brother. We never knew what to call Doll so we just addressed her by her married name, Mrs. Powers.

Dad's brothers and sisters: black, yellow, white, and brindle numbered about twenty–eight that we knew about. Uncle Lincoln and Aunty Pearl remained stoic. They'd been Gran's lifelong friends from the time they used to possum together. Small tears were mopped up quickly.

In the aisle alongside them Uncle Darcy sat in his wheelchair. Someone from AA had come up from Charleville to support him through the funeral so that he didn't get back on the grog. We didn't know what AA meant. Everyone thought Uncle Darcy's staying sober at his mother's funeral was a waste of a really good drinking opportunity and that the AA member was nothing but a nark for stopping him from having a few. Most of the family had made it back to pay their last respects to Gran. It seemed she had no relatives. Vincent, her brother had died from the grog long ago.

Grandfather had a brown and white checked handkerchief in his hand that he dabbed in the corner of his eyes. He'd had them on the barmaid from the Western Hotel for the past week.

35

Aunty Jane, Dad's sister was conspicuous by her absence. Since Grandfather had excised her from the family no one was game to mention her again. She told Dad she didn't want to start a brawl by coming to the funeral.

Aunty Gloria had taken Aunty Pearl with her when they'd sneaked back out to the homestead while Grandfather wasn't there. They'd carefully packed up the pink satin bedspread and silk curtains Gran had lovingly made for her daughter so many years ago on her old treadle sewing machine. They'd brought other mementos of Gran for Jane and hidden them under Aunty Gloria's bed. It was just as well because after the funeral Grandfather'd asked Dad to help him fix the place up. Over the fencing he'd told Dad that he'd sell the place to him. He said the memories were too much. They shook hands on the deal.

Dad worked out there day after day fencing, shearing and mustering while he waited for the finance to come through from the bank.

His father sat on the front verandah in his rocking chair waited on by one of our black cousins. He directed Dad onto the next jobs he needed to do from the comfort of it. It was only after Dad went to the bank to query the length of time the loan was taking he found out Grandfather had already sold the place just before Gran died.

Much later Henry told me that Grandfather had taken off from the town to make a fresh start with the barmaid. The new owners burnt the place down with everything in it. Grandfather had taken what he deemed valuable. Gran's green and white tin paintings lay in the ashes of the old homestead.

The funeral service droned on with nearly everyone saying 'Amen' in the appropriate places or lagging a few seconds behind in case it wasn't. And then Gran's life and the memorial to it was over.

While everyone went out to the burial grounds Aunty Gloria dashed straight home with Aunty Pearl to prepare the food for the wake. Everybody's children went with them. Baby Girl came with me. The kids were told to play in the backyard under the pain of death for any misbehaviour.

Aunty Gloria and Aunty Pearl had more food to get ready before the adults got there. Aunty Pearl threw a large white tablecloth over the dining room table then seemingly out of nowhere Aunty Gloria placed a variety of sponge cakes like Molong, Jew, rose, and ginger in a line down the middle of it. They were elevated on glass cake stands. Petite kiss cakes held together with apricot jam, Lincoln crisps, and raspberry drops were artfully placed on doyley–lined plates. Tiny canapés were daintily displayed in and around the larger morsels so they had the effect of table decorations.

Aunty Pearl and Aunty Gloria then ran back to the kitchen.

Anchovy paste mixed with lemon juice was spread on small toasted squares of bread. Aunty Pearl topped them with finely chopped pickled gherkin. Aunty Gloria brought out the hot cheerios she'd brushed with butter before she baked them in the oven. A toothpick was stuck in each one before she arranged them around bowls of homemade mayonnaise. Once she'd interspersed them with gherkins they made a red, white and green pattern.

Dad and Uncle Harry carried Uncle Darcy into the dining room. Uncle Rhodie came up behind them with his wheelchair. They lifted him off the dining room chair and into his wheelchair. Dad told me to go and get him some water.

I looked at Baby Girl and nodded. She came over to sit out of sight near Uncle Darcy. She could duck under the table once the grog got going and the fights broke out.

The AA member took a chair near Uncle Darcy.

I heard bits and pieces of their conversation. '… courage to change the things I can and the wisdom to know the difference …' they were saying over and over. I took the platters of cheese fingers, some with curried butter as their base, from Aunty Gloria. They'd replaced the empty plates I'd collected before I went into the kitchen. While everyone tucked into the food I went back to the kitchen to get a large glass from the cupboard.

Aunty Gloria was slaving over the hot stove making more hors d'oeuvres and savouries. Dad'd provided the bacon he'd cured for her angels on horseback minus the oysters and most of the other ingredients that would've made it authentic but Aunty Gloria was more than creative. She spread a very thin layer of veal forcemeat over a slice of bacon then she removed the skin from a small cheerio sausage and placed it on top. She rolled it up and secured it with a wooden toothpick. She baked dozens of them in the oven of her old wood stove. Aunty Pearl mixed up biscuits *au diavle*. She whipped grated cheese, chutney, mustard, cayenne pepper, and salt around until she was satisfied with the end result before she piled it up on a buttered biscuit base. They too went into the oven.

'Don't give Darcy just plain water, Jenny.'

Aunty Gloria spoke over her shoulder as she drained a couple of cans of tinned asparagus. She'd buttered thin slices of white bread with the crusts removed ready to place the asparagus on it.

'I've got some lemon barley water in the fridge for him.'

She rolled up the bread and asparagus then fastened them with wooden toothpicks.

'Your mother just adores asparagus,' she said as she fried the rolls in smoking fat until they were brown.

After draining them on white paper she removed the picks, piled the rolls high in a dish lined with a white doyley, sprinkled them with parsley and gave them to one of her children to pass around to the mourners.

I took two jugs of barley water from the kero fridge. I held them in one hand and more food in the other as I made a dash for the table before I dropped them. I'd tried grog when I was in joints in The Valley with the Fairy Man. Beer tasted like soap, wine like tin and spirits like kerosene. After that I filled my glass with water and said it was vodka.

Uncle Lincoln, Uncle Lionel, Dad and his brothers were deep in conversation. Union business. Henry was standing near them as if he too belonged with the men. The AA member poured Uncle Darcy his lemon barley water and then a glass for himself. Everyone felt very sorry for Uncle Darcy.

'Barley water for a rum drinker.' they tutted to each other.

I left the jugs near them in case they wanted some more. Uncle Darcy's daughter sat near Baby Girl. All the kids were slowly moving in under the table. I filled a plate of food up for them and handed it down to Baby Girl. I followed it with glasses of barley water.

Dad broke out of the conversation to catch Mum's eye. '

Why don't you go and give Gloria and Pearl a hand, Rene?'

Mum looked him over in distaste.

'I wasn't born to work in a kitchen.'

She turned her back on him making sure everyone saw her roll her eyes in contempt. Mum's idea of a good spread was a corn beef and mustard pickle sandwich placed elegantly on a Wedgewood plate. We ate it with a heavy silver knife and fork. We polished them every Saturday morning before we did the shopping for the week.

Violetta, the French hairdresser, arrived with a basket filled with bottles of wine she'd bought from Romavilla Vineyards. She greeted Mrs. Cunningham with the French interpretation of her name.

'Bon jour, Mrs. Crazy Bacon.'

No one had the heart to correct her. Most of the town had learned enough French to talk to Violetta's extended family. They accepted the fact that they probably wouldn't do much better in French than she was doing with English. She put the wine on the dining room table then went over to join Mum. They both lit cigarettes.

'See you've still got Rene under your thumb, Tom.'

Uncle Harry noted Mum's behaviour with a sympathetic smile.

Dad had a bit of grog in him and he didn't appreciate it.

Henry did though and it didn't go unnoticed by Dad.

I checked that Baby Girl was still under the table.

I went back into the kitchen to see what I could do for Aunty Gloria. She put the biscuit savouries she'd prepared onto plates. Aunty Pearl had mashed up hard-boiled eggs and chopped parsley then bound it together with Rosella tomato sauce. She sprinkled it with salt and pepper. Other biscuits were topped with cheese with mixed nuts and chutney stirred into it. A few dozen or so had cold boiled ham and raisins bound with salad dressing on them.

The food disappeared as fast as Aunty Gloria and Aunty Pearl could put it on a plate. Finally when they came out into the dining room to see if everyone'd had enough food and drink the mourners told them how wonderful the wake had been. Both Aunty Pearl and Aunty Gloria flushed with pride and embarrassment. Mum looked Aunty Gloria over then turned back to Violetta.

'Trust that Gloria to show off. Can't even contain herself for a funeral.'

Violetta looked shocked but Mum felt by dint of her superior breeding she could say and do whatever she liked to anyone. She loved pointing out the difference between herself and people like Gloria. Gloria, she used to say in faint disgust, sobbed her way through E.V. Timms and shuddered at Carter Brown's crime–ridden novels. Mum on the other hand, being highly cultured and well-bred, read Georgette Heyer's Regency romances, but only for their historical aspects, and Agatha Christie for the more educational. She'd decided long ago that people should consider themselves lucky she deigned to notice them at all.

After a while people began to drift home. They shook Grandfather's hand as they went down the steps and thanked him for the wonderful wake.

Dad collected us and we left too. We walked home through wordless warm dry air. Henry was bursting at the seams in his eagerness to talk to Mum. Dad went out the back to shave some wood to make chips to start the old stove in the morning. Baby Girl sat at the table with her homework. She was whiter than a sheet. Chills went up and down my spine.

Mum was making some tea.

Henry went up to her to speak on the quiet. 'I've got the money.'

'What on earth are you talking about?'

'The money. I've got enough.' Henry was speaking as if nobody knew about his Save Mum fund. 'I've found a place for us to stay as well.'

Baby Girl's eye caught mine. She was frantic. I moved closer to her. Any second it'd be on. I checked out potential weapons and escape routes. Baby Girl was doing the same.

'It's neither the time nor the place, Henry. We've only just buried your grandmother.'

'I have to go back with Uncle Harry tonight. You can finally leave Dad. Just pack a few things. Uncle Harry'll give us a lift to the city.'

'Henry.' I tried to get his attention. 'Henry. Stop it.'

They ignored me.

'What? In that rusty old bucket Harry calls a car? I wouldn't be seen dead in it.'

Dad came in with the chips and the firewood. He put it beside the stove. He was in no mood to be brooked.

'Wouldn't be seen dead in what?' he asked as he poured himself a rum, downed it in one go then poured another. He was already fuller than a boot.

'Harry's car.' Mum's reply had a mocking edge to it that pushed the air upwards into the thick black clouds that'd appeared overhead. 'Henry's under the impression we're going to drive to Brisbane in it.'

Mum brought the teapot over together with a cup and saucer. I drank my tea the same way as Dad did—no milk or sugar.

'Is that a fact?'

Dad sat at the kitchen table near Baby Girl and me. He began to drum his fingers on it.

'It's what Mum has always wanted.' Henry'd become emboldened. 'To go back to the city.'

'Oh really, Henry," Mum snorted in contempt. 'Only you could've taken that seriously. I was just teaching you fiscal responsibility.'

She came back to Dad to put a plate of biscuits in front of him. After she put them down she continued to stand by Dad's side. Mum turned on Henry.

'It was a joke, Henry. It was always a joke. Why on earth would I leave your father?'

She rubbed more salt into Henry's wounds.

'Stop being so stupid and grow up.'

She kept prodding at Dad and Henry trying to trigger an explosion. She was expert in finding the sore spot.

'Your father is a very good provider. Far better than you could ever hope to be.'

Henry looked confused.

'But you said−.'

He trailed off unsure what to do or say next. Saving Mum had been the sole focus of his life ever since he was a little boy. He had no other ambition or purpose. It'd never occurred to him to make other plans or live his own life.

Mum struggled to get her mouth under control. It wouldn't stop smirking. She tried to get her red lipsticked mouth to bow in sorrow to befit the tragic circumstances. It kept turning upwards in a big grin.

I moved my chair back slightly to give me more room. Baby Girl was getting ready as well.

Dad stood up. He looked twice the giant of a man he already was. He was black with rage. He picked Henry up and shook him like a rag doll.

'You can git back to Brisbane right now. I never want to see you again.'

Dad ran Henry down the corridor and speared him into the gravel path outside. Mum made flapping protest noises as she followed them. I got Baby Girl into the bedroom and propped the window up, moved her near it and squeezed out words.

'If this gets any worse BG, go straight out the window and over to The Mish to Uncle Lincoln. Don't risk walking past the house to get to Aunty Gloria. I'll get you from there.'

Henry'd picked himself up. Half the side of his face was peeled raw from the gravel. He made a last silent plea to Mum. She looked at him as if the very sight of him made her sick. Henry went to walk away but found himself alongside Dad's ute. He began to kick its sides in and its signage off. Dad fired several warning shots in and around Henry but he kept kicking the ute as if he'd gone mad.

'Tom, no,' Mum called out dramatically. 'He's not worth it.'

Several neighbours came out to see what was going on. Uncle Harry pulled up at the front gate. He got out of the car, took in the fight and then strolled over to Dad and Henry.

'Got your stuff, champ?' he said to Henry.

I grabbed Henry's bag from the verandah and ran down with it.

Uncle Harry took it from me.

'Well we're all set then. Get in the car, Henry. It's a long drive home.'

Henry snatched his bag and threw it in the back of Uncle Harry's car. Dad still had a bead on him. Henry got in the front passenger seat and slammed the door. Uncle Harry stuck out his hand. Dad was forced to put the rifle down to shake it.

'I guess there'll be no more Christmases.' Uncle Harry pumped Dad's hand then mine. 'So I'll see you in the city.'

Uncle Harry waved at Mum and then ambled back to the car.

With a toot of his horn he drove off.

Dad inspected the damage done to his car.

'Look at that.' He was furious. 'Just flamin' have a look at what he did.'

Henry had kicked the H off the Holden sign. Now it said 'olden. Dad got into it and drove off in the direction of the nearest hotel.

'Come inside.'

Mum was still trying to milk the situation for all it was worth.

'No use in providing any more free entertainment for the neighbours.'

She made sure everyone saw her look tragically one last time down the road in the direction of Uncle Harry's car before she turned on me.

'Thank god they're gone. At least I won't have to listen to your Aunty Bloss whinging to me all the time about your behaviour. She couldn't stand you, you know.'

Mum went up the stairs to the verandah.

'Probably why she gave you all those peculiar clothes to wear. To make you look like the joke that you are.'

She walked down the hallway.

'My father was the master of your father's family and they were nothing more than his servants. I'll never forget it even if they try to.'

Baby Girl's head stuck out from the side of the house. She was shaking from fright; her fingertips bleeding.

'It's all right, BG. It's over.'

'Will Henry ever come back?'

I put my arm around her.

'I don't know BG, but I won't leave you.'

She shook my arm from her shoulders.

'Yes you will. Everyone does.'

Rebel trotted up to her from the back paddock and fell in by her side.

Together they walked down towards the gully to seek shelter under the river gums.

THE BREAKER

The thin blue air burnt my nostrils as I joined a couple of new city staff members on the hospital verandah to see what they were looking at.

Red dust blew up in the cattle yards near the Showground as if someone had dropped a large boulder in it. Once it settled a number of men stood on top of the race ready to release the rider.

'Oh look, here he comes again.'

They'd never seen a horse being broken in by the sounds of things.

'I wonder if his parents know.'

Her friend was gawking this way and that trying to get a better look.

The horse buckled out of the race almost bent in half. A small figure floated over the saddle as the horse twisted this way and that, trying to throw even that light weight off. Both appeared determined to get the better of the other no matter what.

Underneath their Akruba hats gnarled and weather–beaten old men sat on the rails around the yards watching. Without any show of emotion they smoked their rollies as they saw the rider rise in the air and hit the ground. Dust blew up and covered the body for a few seconds. No one sitting on the split rails moved to check or to help.

Baby Girl was deliberately hurting herself as much as she possibly could while looking as if she was doing something else. She was also trying to get the measure of the horse as much as the horse was trying to get hers. The horse was winning. Another breaker ran out to divert the horse away from her with his hat. A couple of men jumped down to grab it to take it back into the yards and load it up again.

'My god that must hurt.'

The new staff member turned to explain what was happening.

'He's been trying to break that horse in all morning. He'll be covered in bruises. Like to hear him try to explain that to his parents.'

Baby Girl dusted herself off then made her way back to the race. After a short while the gate opened again. She came out, one arm in the air and the other on the reins. Her hat flew off and her straw yellow hair stuck up on end. The horse bucked her off. Each time she flew into the air and hit the ground she picked herself up straight away to make her way back to the race. With each ride she retreated more and more into herself, alone and not dependent on anyone. She was disappearing into the dust.

'I can't watch anymore. He's going to end up killing himself. You'd think those men would stop him.'

The new-comers made their way into the darkened interior of the hospital rooms.

Baby Girl rode out again.

I have to go.

The horse twisted every which way to throw her off. She held her arm up in the air again. The horse tried to smash her legs against the railings but Baby Girl quickly jumped into a sidesaddle position the way Greenhide had taught her. Before she could get her legs back over the horse again he tried to scrape her off the saddle but she quickly moved her legs back over the other side. The horse bucked round and round the yard. Baby Girl let him exhaust himself. The horse dropped his head and began to snort heavily towards the ground. Baby Girl kicked her heels into its flanks. The horse tried to put his head up but Baby Girl kept a tight rein on him. He hung his head in defeat.

I have to go. She's going to end up killing herself.

At Baby Girl's urging he began to trot around in a tight circle. The men waited up on the railings, watching as she kicked him into a canter. As she rode around the ring one by one the men began to clap. The horse was like putty in Baby Girl's hands. It'd do anything she asked of it. She raised one arm above her head in triumph as she took the horse back into the yards. She had managed to half kill herself and win at the same time.

It has to stop.

'What are you doing out here, nurse?' The Matron thumped me in the back the way the nuns used to. 'Get inside and wait with the others in the dining room. The Doctor is waiting to give you an anatomy lecture.'

Anger made me taller than she was.

'And pigs might fly.'

'I beg your pardon.'

The Matron was flanked by several important looking men in suits. They were from the Department of Health in the city.

'We've been sitting in that dining room every day for months waiting for a lecture from the doctor, or anyone at all. He never turns up. In fact,' I spoke directly to the men, 'we're never had a lecture from him the whole time I've been here. He's usually too drunk to walk let alone talk.'

'That's enough. You have no right to speak to your superiors unless they have specifically given you permission to address them. Now get inside.'

The Matron'd flushed pink and red.

'No.'

I stood there with my hands on my hips to see what she was going to do. I'd made some more plans while I watched Baby Girl. Julie and several other trainee nurses were peeping out from the hospital ward.

'I'll deal with you later.'

'Better do it now. There won't be a later. I've got other things to do too. We've had no training since I got here. For being on call nearly twenty hours a day seven days a week I'm paid less than ten pounds a fortnight. The only nursing we do is cleaning. Our sleeping quarters—for which you charge me a couple of pounds a week—should be condemned, and our working conditions are horrific. You aren't my superiors or anything else. Not a single one of you is superior to me.'

Shaking with fury I walked down the steps of the hospital.

'I don't need you. I don't need anybody.'

The hard orange streaked white–blue autumn sky hovered over me as I crossed the dry creek bed to get to the river. At The Mish Uncle Lincoln was watching some kids play cricket with the Old People.

He took me in before he drawled, 'Gidday, bubby.'

The Mish was falling to bits. The people here had been told they didn't know how to look after their children so white people were taking them away. They were told they didn't know how to eat the right food so they were banned from eating native food and given, white flour, sugar, salt and fat that was killing them. They had to buy very expensive water with scarce money. They tried to drink away their resentment and sadness. It too had taken them over. Unable to get rid of white people they'd begun to bash and kill to get rid of each other. I wondered how white people thought the blackfellas had lasted over eighty thousand years without their help or perhaps they didn't think at all except about what they wanted. And they wanted the land, by hook or by crook. It was mostly by crook, Dad said.

We watched the cricket match for a while. We smoked our rollies before Uncle Lincoln broke the silence

'When our mob played the British at Lords in eighteen sixty–eight they thought we'd be naked and half-mad because that'd be what blackfellas were. Unaarrimin captained the side. We won fourteen matches, lost fourteen, and drew nineteen. Gave the whitefellas a bit of a fright. Unaarrimin turned pro when he got back but his mob never toured again. The Gov'mint thought of a way to block us from beating whitefellas at their own game. They'll always try to stop you from doing something and you'll always have to figure out a way around it. They never play fair.' He laughed as he slapped his thighs. 'We don't let much get in our way. Neither should you. Got to learn to go round.'

A cheerful argument broke out about whether someone's foot was in or not. One of the Old Fellas ruled it in and the match resumed.

'Heard y'sister was breaking horses down in the yards again.'

Lincoln grunted as he turned to get his billy to put it on the fire.

'It's why I've got to go.'

Uncle Lincoln nodded. 'Where're you off to?'

'I've got a job lined up at Mt Isa. Still nursing. I applied for it a few weeks ago. It should throw Mum and Dad off the scent for a while then I'll make it back to the city. I won't tell them where I am this time so they can't go me again. I've got a fair bit saved. Once I've got a place I'll come back to get Baby Girl. I should be able to agist her horse near the city so she can still be with it. I've got to get her away from Mum before she kills herself.'

I stopped for a second or so before I added, 'God I hate nursing.'

'Kalkadoon mob's up there.'

Lincoln made some tea and stoked up the fire again.

'That fight at Battle Mountain wiped a lot of them out years ago but the last big blue over that way was in nineteen twenty–eight. Several mobs got together to try to drive all the whitefellas out of the Top End. Nearly did too. Bullymen got the better of them—them and the Native Police.'

He stopped so we could clear our throats and spit.

'Made a lot of whitefellas nervous though, the Warramulla. They can't jug all of us to stop us from trying again one day but it seems that they're still having a stab at it. Most of our mob barely get out of jail before they're thrown back in again for having curly hair or something. You know, bubby, they're going to have to come to taws with us one day.'

Uncle Lincoln put some bread on his wire fencing fork and held it over the coals.

'Your father and I were out droving up around the Isa when we were kids.'

He turned the toast over to do the other side.

'Dad told me about the stone cities you'd found down round Augathella.'

Uncle Lincoln was lost in thought for a while.

'We had everything in those days. We were never without food, friends, or water. All the British gave us was the Queen, cricket and the clap.'

He buttered the toast and gave me half.

'Did your father tell you about the well? There's water out there— lots of it if you know where to look. Those desert mobs kept the place spic and span I can tell you. Every mob spent their time taking great care of everything down to the last blade of grass. The law was based around managing the land so we always had food, water and fun. We always had fun. The Dreaming underpinned everything we believed in. Now we're not allowed even touch what was once ours.'

I gave him a hug.

'Dad said some mobs ran in front of the cattle laying down tree branches for them to walk on so they didn't cut up the ground.'

He'd added that the mobs used to cry, howling in ferocious anguish with the pain of the land as the cattle drove their hooves through it. They were the land and the land was them.

The British'd thought the park–like landscape they squatted on was a natural occurrence. They didn't know the blackfellas had fire-stick farmed it to be like that until it was too late and they'd buggered it up.

Instead of being managed by fire the bush now burst into flames as if it were so angry about what had happened to it and its mates, rage was the only emotion it could express. Water flooded the plains in an attempt to drown everything in its path. These days it seemed neither flood nor fire had any respect for anyone let alone themselves. They just went on a rampage whenever they got the chance. There was no one around to help them anymore and the British were never going to ask the blackfellas for advice or knowledge. They'd continued with practices they'd learned in England. It didn't work on this country.

'Everyone kept it so it was like a park. You could walk right around the whole joint. Even Tasmania. The water was well hidden but it was always there. Your father and I, we were out in the central desert when we stumbled across a sandstone well near Lake MacKay. Sandstone blocks.'

We stopped to watch some more cricket.

'The well was round and deep. The markings on it had to be really old because they were the same as the ones on those pyramids I saw in Egypt during the war. It was made out of sandstone blocks too. There was a corkscrew tunnel so someone much smaller than your father or I could slide down into the well to fetch the water. We were going to go back to figure out who made them but we never got around to it. It'd be funny if it was the Egyptians ay?'

Uncle Lincoln chuckled to himself at the memory.

'They used to call the land around here Champagne Country.'

He poured the tea into enamel mugs.

'More like a sly grog shanty now.'

We raised our mugs to each other in salute.

'Will you keep an eye on Baby Girl for me? I'll send you a letter to tell you where I am. Aunty Gloria's going back on the road again with Uncle Rhodie soon so they won't be around.'

'I'll be seeing Rhodie in the march tomorrow,' Uncle Lincoln said by way of agreement.

I drank the rest of the tea and threw the dregs out on the red desert sand. 'I'd better go home. Mum's probably already heard about everything by now.'

'You'll be sweet.'

Uncle Lincoln's assurance gave me some comfort.

'Do you know anyone in the Isa?'

I shook my head. 'I'll only be there a couple of weeks at most. I don't intend to do nursing for a second longer than I have to.'

I bent down to kiss him on the cheek.

He grabbed my hand and squeezed it.

'You got enough money?'

I nodded my head. Uncle Lincoln looked quite anxious. He grabbed my hand.

'Just don't leave the nursing quarters except to go back to the city, will you?'

As I walked away Queenie's son, Arthur, stopped me.

'You going somewhere?'

'Yair. The Isa but I'll be back. I've got to get BG.'

Arthur stretched his thin wiry arms out and wrapped them around me. We hugged each other for a while.

'Just make sure BG is ok for me, will you? I'll be back in a few weeks.'

Arthur released me from his bear hug.

'The Army's going to take me on.' He was bursting with pride. 'I'm going to train to be an electrician.'

'You are so lucky, Arthur.'

We hugged again then I walked away. I slid down the sandy banks of the river then picked my way to the house where Mum was waiting for me. Baby Girl was sitting in the wood heap.

'I'll be back in a minute, ok BG?'

Mum struck a pose at the top of the back stairs by draping herself near the door. Her emerald green dress with turquoise piping around the sleeves and neckline matched her green stilettos. She always looked the goods no matter what was going on.

'The Matron's already called me. You get back up to the hospital and apologise this instant.'

'I've got a job nursing in Mt Isa. I've transfer the time I've served here up there to them.'

'You're not going anywhere.'

'I'm going in the morning.'

Mum walked into the kitchen.

'The only thing you are going to do is what you are told for once.'
When she came back she had Dad's rifle in her hands.

'I don't care if you shoot me.'

I walked towards the rifle barrel until it stuck in my stomach. I grabbed it and twisted it out of her hands.

'I never want to hear from you or Dad for that matter ever again. Happy now? You've only got Baby Girl left to get rid of.'

Mum began to scream at me to get out and live in the gutter like the guttersnipe I was and that I was never to come back. It suited me.

I walked down to Baby Girl to reassure her.

'I'll come by tonight, BG. I want you to promise you'll just stick to riding Rebel at the pony club. I want you in one piece when I get back.'

Baby Girl hung her head. I put my hand under her chin. She was bruised from head to foot.

'Promise.'

She looked away.

'Get inside, you,' Mum snarled from the top steps.

Baby Girl got up slowly. She was hurting quite badly but she wasn't going to show it. She walked up to the steps then sat down to bag her feet.

At the hospital I rolled my swag, bandaged my money around my waist. It was nearly dark when I went down to the creek where Old Bill had his humpy. He lived closer to Dad's house than Uncle Lincoln's mob did.

Old Bill was lying back in an antique saddle he'd thrown on the ground. He had a roaring fire going and a billy on the boil. The camp smelled of sweet damper and stew. He was reading Shakespeare by the firelight. Classical music poured exquisite notes from his battery radio.

'Oh it's you, Jen.'

He peered at me in mild surprise as I came into his camp.

'Just need to wait until it gets darker, Bill.'

He didn't think it was out of the ordinary that I was there. Nothing surprised Old Bill very much.

I moved closer to his fire, swung my swag down to the ground then sat down on a log opposite him. It got quite cold very quickly when the sun went down. Old Bill had to be over a hundred by now but then I thought he might've always looked like that.

It struck me that I hardly knew who anybody was. I wished I had more time to talk to him; to ask him who he was; why he was here; how he got here or where he came from. I wanted to ask all of them who they were. They'd been in the background of my life making it what it was for sixteen years.

I'd run out of time.

Old Bill began to read aloud from his battered book in a magnificent Scottish burr.

'Tomorrow and tomorrow and tomorrow creeps in this petty place from day to day; to the last syllable of recorded time.'

I joined in with him.

'And all our yesterdays have lighted fools the way to dusty death. Out, out, brief candle!'

We recited Macbeth together.

'Life's but a walking shadow, a poor player that struts and frets his hour upon the stage and then is heard no more. It is a tale told by an idiot, full of sound and fury, signifying nothing.'

We finished in laughter.

'I wrote that in my autograph book at school. Everyone else was writing roses are red, violets are blue, nuns stink, and so do you.'

The last memory I had of leaving the convent made me smile, that and the added glee of knowing that half of it had burnt down a few days later.

'You are quite welcome to put your swag down here for the night.'

Old Bill still retained his country courtesy and courtly manners.

'Thanks, Bill. I just have to see if Baby Girl's alright then I'll be back.'

'Take your time, Jen. I'll save some grub for you.'

Everyone's dogs barked all along the road as I made my way to Baby Girl's window. Along with the rifle, Dad had also given Mum the red dog to guard her so she felt safer. It was on its back with its legs in the air and its head thrust back so it could get maximum attention. I stroked it on the tummy and under the chin before I tapped on glass to get Baby Girl to let me in.

The moonlight illuminated her body. It was turning yellow and green. She limped back to bed. I sat on the edge of it.

'I'm not deserting you. I'm only going to be in Mt Isa for a couple of weeks to top up my money and to throw Mum and Dad off the scent. After that I'll hitch down to Brisbane. I'll see if Henry will put me up, if not, it doesn't matter. I've saved up enough to rent something. Once I've settled in and got another job, I'll come back for you. Brisbane has heaps of stables and I'll find somewhere to agist Rebel. I'll be a month at the most. If things get bad here, go over to Uncle Lincoln. He will know where I am. He'll look after you. It's the best I can do BG. I'm so sorry.'

She put her small hand with her bleeding and chewed fingertips into mine. I held it until she pulled it away.

'And please BG, stay safe.'

There was no reply.

I gave her a quick kiss on her forehead. She made a big display of scrubbing it off with the top of the sheet. I went back down to the creek where Old Bill greeted me with a cup of tea and some hot food. We talked into the night about poetry, books and music.

After a few hours' sleep it was time to go.

Old Bill picked up a hessian bag with his day's provisions in it, then swung his axe up on his shoulder in readiness for work. His tattered old dungarees were held up with rope. He'd plonked a scruffy hat full of holes on his head. His bushy white beard went down to his waist, covering a faded shirt.

With my swag over my shoulder I walked with him into town.

Everyone was lined up to see the march down to the War Memorial.

The Returned Soldiers League or the RSL who helped those who'd served in the war had also ended up in politics. The conservative anglophiles who worshipped the monarchy imposed the idea that only they represented Australian culture and the White Australia Policy was the only philosophy we needed. The armed forces, represented by the RSL, and religion enforced it and the Menzies regime ran the country on it.

The women who'd fought in the war stood on the sidelines. They didn't get a look in after the war because they were banned from just about anything it was possible to ban them from. They couldn't be a member of a club, hold a job if they were married, have their own bank accounts, own property, go into a hotel by themselves, or do or say anything else that might have cast aspersions on the prowess of their men or encroached on male territory.

"Or get them to share power." The Mad Goat Lady from One Mile Creek would always add her two bob's worth to the conversation. "So much for fighting for freedom. Not ours, that's for sure." And she laughed and laughed.

They also banned women from most sporting events, being jockeys or anything else they could think of. The government told women they'd made all these rules to prevent them from damaging their reproductive organs. It was for their own good. It was most certainly not to stop women being the equal of men. After all this is Australia—the Land of the Fair Go.

The drummer in the town's band hit the skins with his sticks. The men shuffled into their ranks.

Uncle Rhodie'd ended up as a biscuit bomber, dangling dangerously out the side of a plane aiming provisions down to the troops. If he saw the Japanese he aimed anything else he could lay his hands on. He never talked about what he did but he had a lot of medals.

The Government'd stopped shearers from joining up as they were now essential services so Dad just kept working in the sheds. He got a white feather every year for his efforts.

Uncle Rhodie adjusted his hat.

It was sitting at a smart–arsed angle that sent shivers down Aunty Gloria's spine.

Scattered applause rippled across them as Uncle Rhodie led the Anzac Day parade down the main street.

The town's brass band blared out the Colonel Bogey march. Uncle Lincoln and his mob tramped closely behind Uncle Rhodie. Their boots stuck on the new bitumen. Uncle Darcy wheeled his chair alongside them. His medals glistened in the sunshine. Uncle Rhodie got into the swing of things and began to sing out over the thumping feet.

'Bullshit! That all the brass could say.' He bawled on top note over the brass band. 'Bullshit! They fed us night and day.'

'Rhoo-dieeee,' Aunty Gloria called out from the crowd. 'That's enough.'

Uncle Rhodie's grin slipped up the side of his face. He'd won that skirmish and, once the march was over, the men would go down to the pub where the real fight would begin. It never changed from year to year. Graziers versus Shearers. Liberals versus Labor. Conservatives versus the working people. Black versus White. Communists versus everyone.

I tried to imprint them all into my brain.

A chilly wind blew through and I shivered.

Perhaps I wouldn't see them again.

Uncle Freddie was selling The Tribune on the street corner, the sole protestor.

'You've been done like a duck's dinner, comrades. Menzies went to Germany to shake Hitler's hand on behalf of his fellow Aryans. So did Joe Lyons. Menzies said that no one'd care about Hitler invading Poland. He told Churchill that no one gave a tinker's curse about Singapore either. Menzies tried to appease Hitler. He's adapted him and his ideas to rule us.'

'Now he tells us,' someone muttered alongside me. 'After the flamin' election.'

Uncle Freddie yelled over the band as the men tramped past.

'Eat everyone else first was Menzies motto. Leave me til last. Read all about it.'

He waved his Tribune in the air.

Menzies had won the last election but only by a small margin. People were losing their fear of being told what to think, called communists, being told how to vote by the media, condemned by the church or thrown out of a job by their employers if they voted for the Labor Party.

Menzies'd twiddled his thumbs from election to election for over fifteen years. He only had one policy—calling ordinary people communists at election time. He'd been a lawyer once but the only job he'd held since before the war and afterwards was being a parliamentarian. It was paid for by the taxpayers he vilified.

Dad'd given a short snort.

"Menzies and his mob will do or say anything the British or the Yanks ask. No pride that bloke. Typical boozer. Democracy be blowed."

I walked past the last of the trees in the gidgee woodland.

Uncle Lincoln and his mob used its leaves to smoke ghosts away but everybody else made fence posts out of them.

As there was little traffic I got my most prized possession out from my coat pocket—a grey, black and white trimmed transistor radio.

Hank Williams's lonesome blue voice rolled down the road with me.

On the edge of the gravel highway I stuck my thumb out as I walked along to make my way to the airport in Charleville a few hundred miles away.

THE LUCKY DOOR PRIZE

A giant silver aeroplane sat on the tarmac.

I'd only seen them in movies.

They usually had a romantic mist wafting around them while an orchestra softly played underneath the throbbing engine as a lovelorn couple said goodbye.

Planes were also the last word in luxury.

In magazines the plush dark velvety seats invited you to sink into them while immaculately dressed hostesses, glamorously holding a shiny serving tray in one hand, dispensed long cool black and white drinks with the other.

The captain'd always dress in a snowy white homage to the armed services.

Henry told me once the trim on their caps and shoulders was made out of real gold. Unlike Uncle Rhodie's hat, their caps were always placed squarely on their heads, ready to march in triumph to wherever life took them.

The ticket had cost a lot of money but I had to be in the Isa by tomorrow to report for work. It was a thousand miles up north.

Before I could get any closer a brown whirly wind wound around it then twirling wildly left the tarmac to go bush. The plane was covered in dust and curses. Legs and a few bare feet were on the other side. I was unsure whether I should get on it.

A big mob of well-dressed blackfellas had gathered near a large opening in the side of the plane. They must've come down for ceremony or obligation or maybe a rodeo. The whirly wind hadn't bothered them.

The captain had a quick glance at my ticket.

He was dressed in stained moleskins with a tattered old shirt tucked in the front but forgotten at the back where a bottle of Johnny Walker stuck out of the pocket. With a wave of his cigarette he directed everyone to pitch in to throw parcels and goods into the plane.

When he pushed his Akubra hat back to observe how well we were doing, I saw that he had tried to stick what hair he had to his scalp with Brylcreem. He took frequent swigs from the bottle before he was finally satisfied we'd loaded everything properly.

He locked the hold down, got out the bottle again, had a long swig, put it away, and gestured for us to follow him up the stairs.

"Steadying m'nerves," Dad used to call it.

'I'll be as right as rain as soon as I sit down.' He staggered inside. 'Too bloody blotto to stand for much longer anyhow.'

My eyes adjusted to the dark interior.

The inside of the plane was stacked with mailbags, sacks of potatoes, rice, flour and other goods. As the blackfellas'd gone through the door they'd grabbed a giant blue–green pumpkin from the pile that had been stored inside the doorway. There was no seating.

'Better hold a pumpkin, luv.'

An old blackfella rolled a large Queensland blue towards me as the plane took off down the runway.

I didn't get a chance to put my swag down to sit on before I fell on my bum.

They all laughed then everyone yelled in unison.

'Take off.'

Each had put a pumpkin on their lap. The kids sat on top of them and gummed themselves to the front of the adults. As seasoned travellers they hung on for grim death. I put the pumpkin on my lap as I struggled to stay on the floor.

The Namatjirra painted land changed itself into enchanted purple ranges on a yellow and green savannah. Tiny trees were scattered here and there as we rode the air in an endless blue sky. We rose higher and higher into a world of clouds. They stepped around the sun, then wrapped themselves around an empty white moon daubed with a bit of black, before dipping and diving in front of us for a while. They flew away to leave us in blue.

The pilot fortified himself with some more grog.

God popped into my mind. Feeling a bit cramped I shifted myself around and managed to stand up.

'Better not, luv.'

The old blackfella warned me.

After I sat and put the pumpkin on top of me again the plane plummeted. Its contents hit the ceiling. We were having trouble remaining on the floorboards.

'Air pocket,' the blackfellas yelled obviously enjoying themselves.

The pilot got the plane back up into the air again. The contents fell down, missing us by inches. I decided that if this were the end, there was no going back. I'd stick with atheism.

The pilot yelled out something about hanging on because he was going to land. Through the tiny front window, there was nothing but red dirt for as far as the eye could see. The pilot skidded into it while we clung onto our pumpkins. He opened up the door, shoved some stairs down and we climbed out. A few emus were still running for their lives.

After we rolled some smokes and had a few puffs, we began to unload bags of provisions and mail. On the horizon we could see a tiny ball of dust approaching. Some golden coloured dingoes stood up on a small red ridge to check us out. A few crows flew overhead. We huddled under the plane wings to get a bit of shade. The kids ran in and under the plane's belly playing tag.

Eventually the truck pulled up. A waterbag swung from the front of it. The kids took turns at putting their mouths under the water that dripped from it. The driver got out of the cabin and strolled over. He was a rangy man, well-built with a large stained brown Akubra hat shading his face, moleskin trousers, riding boots and an old faded blue-checked shirt. His wife and kids stayed in the cabin staring at us. He tipped his hat back on his head a little before he shook hands with the pilot. We began to load his goods up on the back of the truck. When we finished the man got back in his truck and, with a wave, drove off. We all rolled another cigarette, had a mug of water then got back in the plane.

We must've landed and taken off half a dozen times or more to deliver mail and provisions before we lurched down the tarmac at Mt Isa. The blackfellas neatly stacked their pumpkins up near the door as they left. A few utes and dogs greeted their arrival. After unloading their goods from the plane they piled in the back of the utes. With a wave they drove off.

I swung my swag over my shoulder and followed the pilot's direction to get to the hospital. The heat was stifling. The Matron showed me the staff quarters. She informed me the kitchen was closed and I would have to wait until morning to get something to eat. I opened up a cupboard. My uniforms were already hanging in the wardrobe. I hated them on sight. After I put my swag down I decided to see if I could get something to eat while it was still daylight.

Hotels made up a rough and ready street. Men hung out of the crowded windows with schooners of beer in their hands. As I walked down it looking for a café they whistled, hooted, hollered and shouted obscene comments at and about me. The wall of abuse pushed me back out towards the road.

This is dangerous. Violent. Ten times more people here than at home.

A couple of police were on the other side of the road. People stepped off the footpath to let them past.

Why are they scared of the coppers?

A blackboard menu caught my eye. The hotel dining room was serving sausages and chips only.

I'm starving.

As was the custom for women, I had to pay full price for only half the portion of food that was served to men.

The Mad Goat Lady from One Mile Creek had reminded us all in an enraged tone about the practice. "And after fighting alongside them in the war, not only are we shunted to one side to do all their dirty work but we're expected to subsidise their bloody food and lodgings as well."

A band warmed up next door to the café.

As I went in to listen to it for a few seconds a woman gave me a ticket that also acted as the lucky door prize. I stood against the wall near the exit sign. The place was packed to the rafters.

After a short time I became aware that someone was standing beside me. He was taller than Dad so he had to be over six foot four but he was just as lithe and lean from hard work. With blue–green eyes, fair hair and lightly tanned skin he was the most handsome man I'd ever seen—not that I'd seen many. When he spoke to me my heart began to pound and my stomach fluttered. I felt sick.

What is the matter with you?

He was very well dressed and he appeared to extremely well-spoken in the way that well-educated people are.

I had difficulty breathing.

Stupid. Stupid. Stupid.

'Would you like to dance?'

But before I could say "I don't dance" I was on the shiny polished wooden floor desperately trying to hang on and not slip over in the sawdust.

He introduced himself as Rupert. I managed to say in gasping breaths that my name was Jenny. He came from Brisbane and worked in the mines to finance his studies. I told him I wasn't staying in Mt Isa long as I was making my way to Brisbane to continue with music and writing. He told me his father had deserted his mother so he helped provide for her and his siblings.

I can't find my body.
My mouth won't shut up.
My heart's drowning out the drummer.

I'm telling him I'm starting work as a nurse tomorrow. Rupert is telling me he's a Catholic then he's asking me what religion I am. I shrug then say I don't have any. He insists I must have one. I tell him I'd been educated in convent boarding schools but when I left them I'd left the church behind as well. I didn't intend to go back. Rupert too was in the process of deserting the Church. He is very interested in Russian literature and Engels. I've read most of the Russian writers. He seems pleased we have so much in common.

I'm scared. It must be getting dark outside. The hospital has a curfew.

In answer to his question and in a desperate attempt to calm myself down, I tell him I'm a Marxist.

'Outside of a dog a book is a man's best friend.' I quote breathlessly. 'Inside of a dog it's too dark to read.'

Rupert frown slightly. 'I don't recall Marx saying that.'

'It was Groucho.'

A small shadow crossed Rupert's face before his smile lit it up. 'That's very clever. You had me going there for a while.'

The dance floor split in two.

Rupert waltzed me over to a wall.

Hide your body. Quickly.

I folded my arms in front of me.

The band stopped playing.

Two peroxided blonde white women, one with long stringy hair, and the other with a beehive were circling each other on the dance floor. They had butcher's knives in their hands. Screaming they ran at each other, plunged the knives in and gutted each other. Their white green innards spilled red and brown down their dresses. To cheers and applause two beer–gutted white men strolled out from the crowd. They acknowledged the crowds as if they were prizefighters who'd just won a bout—their hands were clasped and their arms were raised over their heads. They each picked a woman up and walked outside with her.

Rupert escorted me over to the corner he'd found me in. 'They've been sleeping with each other's husbands. It's been on for weeks.'

A couple of Aboriginal cleaners came in with mops, buckets and brooms to clean the blood up.

A band member tapped the microphone. 'And there's more excitement, folks, yes it's time to draw the lucky door prize.'

He was holding a hat crammed with tickets.

The drummer hit a prolonged drum roll.

'And it's number 69.' The band member announced. 'Number 69.'

People checked their tickets and, failing to win, threw them on the floor for the blackfellas to pick up.

Rupert took the crumpled sweat soaked ticket out of my hand.

'Do you want me to pick it up for you?'

I nodded my head.

Rupert made his way up to the podium. He handed the ticket over, shook the band member's hand then to scattered applause, he made his way back. He was holding a giant leg of pork.

'Do you want me to walk you home with it?'

I took the lucky door prize from him and forced myself to override my usual first thought to agree to whatever anyone said while I plotted flight.

'No. It's ok. I have to go anyway. It was nice meeting you.'

I walked unsteadily through the crowd with the leg of pork. All thoughts of a dignified exit were gone. After I orientated myself out on the darkened footpath I began to walk back to the hospital. I figured even with a ten–ton leg of pork in my hand I could still outrun a drunk or use it to fell an attacker. All I had to do was stay in the middle of the footpath to avoid any ambush from the trees until I got back to the nurses' quarters. I also had to get out of here as fast as I could. Rupert caught up with me. I jumped in fright.

'I'm sorry if I scared you. It's just that we're having a swim and a barbeque lunch tomorrow. I just checked. My friends said it'd be alright if you want to come. There'll be a dozen or so of us. We're meeting at the pool."

I didn't see any friends.

You weren't looking for any.

I feel sick.

It'll be during the day.

I nodded.

'I'll pick you up from here around nine or so. We generally just have a swim then we have a something to eat later.'

I made my way around the corner and almost ran back to the hospital. As I put the leg of pork into the fridge one of the staff wandered over to me.

'Where did you get that?'

'It's the lucky door prize.'

'Lucky alright. We'll cook it tomorrow for lunch.'

As I lay in the dark I thought about Rupert, the leg of pork and the fact I'd agreed to the second date I'd ever had in my life.

He'll see you in swimming togs.
Why didn't you think before you said you'd go?
Talk about stupid. You take the cake.
Maybe there will be so many people around in swimming togs he won't notice me in mine.
Maybe I should just tell him I am sick but then I'd have to see him to tell him.
I don't have a telephone number.
I don't know his last name.
Maybe you should do something without worrying about making a mistake or worse, making a fool of yourself.
I'll concentrate on getting as much money together as I can and head towards Brisbane as I'd planned.
Baby Girl is relying on me.
Maybe the leg of pork is a sign my luck has changed for the better.
Maybe the town isn't as violent and scary as I think it is.
It'll be during the day time.

Over breakfast several girls at the hospital discussed the leg of pork and the previous night. They encouraged me to go out with Rupert. They'd seen him around town. He didn't appear to be a drinker and he was very good looking. I was really lucky they said.

I put on my swimming togs first then carefully pulled all my clothes over the top of them, dabbed on a tiny amount of makeup so I didn't look like mutton dressed up as lamb or as if I was asking for it and went to wait outside for Rupert.

He rode up on a Harley Davidson motorbike with a helmet that completely covered his face.

I'd thought he'd have a car. I should've asked. Stupid.

I'd only seen a couple of motorbikes in my life mainly in magazines. I'd never ridden on one. It seemed that everything conspired against me when it came to a dignified date. I hesitated trying not to panic.

I have no idea what to do.
My sheath skirt won't allow me to get on the seat.
I want to run.

'Just get on the back and hold onto me,' Rupert yelled over the top of the revving motor.

The skirt had corseted my legs. Shame swept over me. I couldn't hear myself think. I'd worn the wrong clothes. I'd never ever held onto anybody in my life or ever touched anyone for any more than five seconds.

'It's not that difficult.'

Rupert voice was muffled by the helmet. He sounded fed up.

I pulled my skirt up slightly and managed to get on the bike. I put my towel and bag between Rupert's body and mine then gingerly clutched his leather jacket with one finger and a thumb.

'You'll have to hold onto me around my waist.'

Rupert gunned the bike then took off at full speed. I clutched his jacket, terrified and then I quickly became disoriented. The bush flew past in a blur. The sun burned down on my body despite the breeze kicked up by the bike.

'It's not too far away.' Rupert slightly turned his head so I could hear him. 'We'll be there in a few minutes.'

I could see the speedometer. Fifty. Sixty. Ninety. Hundred. There was bird sound in the slipstream. I couldn't hear what they were saying. The wind cut into my eyes. The roadway gravel stung my legs. I was becoming panic–stricken. I could see people down by the lake. He sped past them.

'Go back.' I tried to get my mouth to work against the wind. 'Go back.'

He accelerated until we were almost skidding down the road.

I began to hit his back. 'Stop. Turn around.'

My heart was in my mouth.

'It's ok. My friends are just near here.' He drove the bike into a thick scrub before he turned the engine off. 'There's nothing to worry about. The lake's just down there. Christ, anyone's think you'd never done this before.' He took off his helmet.

I struggled to get off the bike and to speak over my fear. 'I haven't.'

He laughed cynically. 'That's what they all say.'

'I want to go back to the hospital.'

My body.

It's run away.

It's left me behind.

Bird song rifled through the water reeds. I don't understand what they're saying.

I can't breathe.

Sick.

Heart pelting.

Blacking out.

Rupert's face filled with rage. He had one hand around my throat and the other holding the front of my shirt. He shook me violently.

'I'm sick of this. What are you trying to be? A virgin? I know you Catholic bitches. You're all sluts. Every last one of you. Always begging for it then pretending you weren't.'

He grabbed my arm and twisted it up my back, then with the other hand began to rip my skirt off. He stopped when he realised I had swimming togs on.

'I don't believe it. You actually thought we were going swimming?' He laughed. 'Fucking Catholic prick teaser. I'll teach you to be smarter than me. You'll think twice about having a smart mouth after I've finished with you.' He was whipping himself up into frenzy. 'You knew what I wanted at the dance. That's all you catholic bitches think of and talk about. Stop lying about it and pretending this is your first time.' He ripped the crutch out of my togs and pushed me face first into the gravel. 'I can do whatever I like to you. See?' He put his knee in my back to pin me down. I could hear him pulling his trousers down.

My body is sliced open.
Salty bloody swirls in my mouth.
Silenced.

'You're all the same. Enjoy it, you bitch. You made me do it.'

He turned me over and belted my head into the ground while he ground himself on top of me.

A spray of silver shooting stars fell in front of me.

'Enjoy it, bitch. Enjoy it.'

He bashed my face over and over.

'Don't you make me feel bad. Stop looking at me like that. You're the one who thought they were better than me. You asked for it.'

He gave a long scream then grabbed me by the hair and pulled me to my feet. He ran me through the bush to the lake.

'I don't see any blood, bitch.'

The people were on the other side of the kale. A long way away.

'If you were really a virgin, there'd be blood. Don't tell me. You did a lot of horse riding when you were little. That's what you're going to tell me, isn't it?'

He threw me into the lake.

'Swim. That's what you said you wanted to do. Swim. Go on.'

He hauled me out of the water again.

'You'll call the cops as soon as I let you go, won't you? I'm not going to jail.'

He began to hit himself in the side of the head.

'You'd like that, wouldn't you? To see me do time for murder as well as rape.'

I finally had a word for what had just happened to me. Rape. Rape and pillage. It was in the history books I read at school. I never knew what it meant. There were only pictures of soldiers carrying off goods and chattels.

Rupert grabbed me.

'Get back on the bike. I'll take you home.'

"You never call the coppers not even if you are on your last legs." I heard Dad say.

Rupert gunned the bike. Sixty. Seventy. One hundred.

'I'll kill both of us. I'll kill both of us. That way no one will know what happened.'

My skin scraped the highway. Laughter. Light. Laughter. Lake. Light. Trees streamed by. Time. Still morning.

'I'm not going to jail. I'm not going to jail. You made me do it. You put the idea into my head. You came on to me. Begging for it.'

Houses. Town. Police station. He drove up to it.

'Go on. Tell them. They won't believe you. It'll be your word against mine. They'll believe me because they know what you Catholic bitches are like.'

You never dob to a copper. Not even if you was on your last legs. Never go near a copper. My face was throbbing. My back twisted in agony. My body was swelling.

'I'll tell them how you led me on.'

Rupert gunned the bike again.

I was back in a Catholic Church again.

A priest stood in front of me.

'Where did he touch you?'

Blood came out of my mouth instead of words.

'You have been extremely wicked, haven't you? You inflamed him. He could have the pick of any girl in this town. Why would he want you? His mother is as devout as he is and every bit as respectable. You are licentious. That's why you got him to do what he did. The nuns taught you that you had free will. You could've stopped him at any time but you didn't. I bet you didn't even try to cross your legs, did you? Or press your knees together. That's because you wanted it. No man can trust you. No decent man will have you. Rupert, despite what you did to him, is willing to marry you. He will be your only offer. I advise you to take it.'

Rupert thanked the priest profusely.

He threw me on the back of the motorbike and drove me back to the hospital.

'I'll see you tomorrow and we can make arrangements. Have your things packed.'

He's so well spoken, well educated.

In a flashy kind of way, Mum conceded.

I wrapped my towel around me, and started to shuffle inside. I was filled with gravel and shame. It was still daytime.

Rupert grabbed my arm again and slightly twisted it just to remind me of the power he thought he held over me.

'I could make a fortune out of you.'

He was threatening me while looking as if we were sharing a joke. He smiled.

'Most of the men in this town would pay me a week's wages to get a piece of you just once. What do you think of that? And don't think you can run away. I'll find you. I can kill you if I want to. I'll get off. No one cares about you. I own you now, you're mine, you can't have another man other than me and don't you forget it.'

Mum used to smile too, just in case anyone was watching.

Were there more than one of her around?

'And don't tell anyone either.'

The sun was still shining.

I tried to sit on the side of my bed but it was too painful. I lay down. Mum said I had free will too. I got it when I was born but I don't think I ever knew what it was, not really. They were right. I was stupid; a boofhead; worthless.

Someone knocked on the door.

'We've cooked the pork. You'd better come and get your share.'

'Save some for me.'

The few words caused the blood to bubble in my throat. All through the night I desperately want to urinate but only small drops of blood came out.

In the morning I shuffled down to the dining room with my swag and picked up the local paper. I looked over the form guide.

Some nurses were congregated together glancing anxiously my way.

I knew what I looked like. The gravel rash had started to form pustules in each puncture wound. I knew they knew. I'd spent hours trying to scrub it off in the shower but I remained covered in it.

The date on the newspaper seemed familiar.

My lips were split. My mouth could hardly move. I picked up my swag. Someone directed me to a bookie's house a few streets away. I dragged my legs along the footpath. Searing pain ripped through my body and a few more drops of bloody urine came out. I'd put a sanitary pad there to catch them.

Feeling feverish I asked the bookie for the odds on Bush Bonanza. He quoted me a hundred to one.

There had to be a fix in.

I put everything I had on it to win. Bush Bonanza came in by a nose. I stuffed the winnings in the bank I carried around my waist, swung my swag up over my shoulder and shuffled down to the highway.

A truck slowed to pick me up.
I threw my swag in and slowly hauled myself in after it.
The driver didn't say anything about my appearance.
'Brisbane alright?'
And he rolled his rig down the highway without waiting for a reply.

WRONG SIDE OF THE ROAD

'You too young to be here.'
The Italian woman who owned the doss house in The Valley in Brisbane hesitated to rent me a room.
'This place only for drunks and showies.'
Her black hair was piled into a bun. A snowy white apron covered her sensible floral dress. Her black stockinged legs were inserted into black sensible shoes. Eventually she got out a key. She showed me to a clean room.
'Where you parents?'
I dug my fingernails into the side of my arm then shrugged. She listened to a lifetime of avoidance so she left me to it.
The room just fitted in a single bed, a tiny cupboard and an even smaller mirror. I sat down to catch my breath.
The Italian woman came back with a plate of food— layers of warm and hearty mincemeat, potatoes, peas and cheese in a pie she baked every day. It was served on a chipped enamel plate. I hadn't eaten for days.
After she left, through the flimsy partitions I listened to men cough their lungs out. I opened the window slightly to let some air in then dialled my radio around to find the sounds of the city in it.
Love songs filled the air. They weren't written for me.
I was too ashamed to go to Henry or Uncle Harry and Aunty Bloss. Mum'd said they didn't like me anyway. I didn't have the confidence to find out if that was right or not.
The truck driver'd told me about the doss house. Everyone who lived on the road knew about it and used it at one time or another.
The next day I covered my face with makeup and my body as much as I could before I drifted down the streets. I'd look for the licensee's name on hotels, walk in, ask for them by name as if I knew them and then try to get a job as anything from them—a cleaner, a waitress, a barmaid.
One owner asked me if I could use a fork and spoon.
'Of course.'
I was eager to impress.

'I can use a knife as well.'

He dumped a burning silver tray full of food in my left hand and a fork and spoon in my right. He fired me after five minutes when he saw me scrape the food off the tray with them. Dad'd fired me all the time so I was quite used to it. I went back to the doss house in the Valley clutching a couple of dollars for a few minutes' worth of work.

I spun my money out by eating the Italian woman's food, and filling up with water until I finally got a job in an office writing up valuations for a real estate agent. I stayed in the doss house because it was cheap and I needed to get more money together.

I sent postcards to Uncle Lincoln to give to Baby Girl so that I could pretend everything was okay. I'm sure he knew they weren't.

The valuer showed me how to draw up plans and make estimates. On my first payday the accountant went to the bank with me to sign the papers so I could have my own bank account.

I was very proud of my small grey bank book and banked whatever I could every week. I always kept some cash in my purse just in case. I tried to put my life back together. With no piano to play, I'd changed my direction into writing. I began to write down the life that was happening to and around me. I enrolled to finish high school by correspondence so I could go to university. I wrote to tell Uncle Lincoln again to say I'd be a few more weeks and to tell Baby Girl I hadn't forgotten about her. I'd be there soon.

On my way home after the office closed I went past a coffee shop called The Primitif. The Purple Hearts played in the window of it. Lobby Lloyd's guitar reverberated down Queen Street. It rattled the high–rise office block windows and shook the walls in my room. It drove the numbness away with its rhythm and blues.

One night I followed a tantalising, fragrant scent up and down Brisbane streets trying to find out what it was and where it came from. I finally tracked it down to a small dark wood–panelled café filled with people of Asian heritage.

On impulse, and feeling slightly foolish, I went in and sat down. The staff didn't know what to do with me. I didn't really know what to do either. We didn't know how to speak to each other. I sat there in the hope they would feed me the heavenly scented food I saw them pick up from a dumb waiter at the back to distribute to the other diners. I noticed they picked up two red sticks to eat it with.

A pot of tea and a tiny china cup patterned with a blue fish was placed in front of me. The tea was a fragrant yellow–greenish colour. I was only used to the black billy brew from Bushels.

Soon the waitress brought over a plate of rice with tiny vegetables in it. The rice at the convent was usually a thick gelatinous gloop cooked in slightly sour milk and filled with sugar to disguise the taste. Nutmeg was always grated on top. Spaghetti was served the same way. I hated sugar and everything with milk in it. But this rice smelled like toast, and each vegetable shone like a jewel. I never knew you could eat rice with vegetables.

Next they brought a plate of very spicy chicken over. Christmas was the only time we ate chicken at home. The waitress pointed to several sugar bowls then handed me two red sticks. I lifted the lids on the pots. One was filled with slices of red and green chili, others had various sauces. I put a dab of each on my plate. I stabbed the food with one of my sticks.

I'd never have to eat boarding school food again.

I went to the cafe every night.

Each time they would bring something different. I was lost in aromatic soups, sweet–scented noodles, crunchy vegetables, meats that melted in my mouth and seafood sprinkled with tiny white, black or brown seeds.

However despite my good food fortune, a growing knowledge of how to use a chopstick, a job and a roof over my head, a warning wind blew in from the west tugging at me from all sides. It forced me to walk quickly back to the doss house for shelter. I turned my radio on.

After the ABC fanfare heralded the evening news the announcer stated in stark British tones there was a dingo drive underway at the town. They were looking for a young girl who was missing in the bush. She'd been gone for over a week. There were fears for her safety. Blacktrackers had been brought in from The Alice to help the locals.

I ran to the pay phone on the footpath outside the doss house door. I was breathless. My heart was beating out of my chest.

'When we get our hands on her we'll belt her senseless for disgracing us like this.' Mum hissed down the line. 'We'll never be able to hold our heads up in this town again. What is wrong with you kids?'

'Would you rather we were dead?'

'That's right. Take her side.'

I hung up, ran back inside, packed my money, a small swag, and raced down the hill to the railway station. Baby Girl had to be out at Grandfather's old place. We knew it like the back of our hand. If she'd been gone a week then she was digging for water in the river sands. Food didn't matter. We could last for weeks without food and sometimes did.

With a few minutes to spare I caught the Westlander. I looked out the window as we left the city. The tiny lights that twinkled in the towns got smaller and smaller the further away we got from the city. They'd run out of electricity by the time we crossed the mountains. Then the carbide lights took over.

The train took all night to meander through the bush then, sensing the Outback, it picked up speed.

Baby Girl can't stay at the doss house.

Maybe Henry can help us.

You haven't seen him since his row with Dad.

White stars created a massive spray in the dark blue sky.

I couldn't bring Baby Girl to the city just yet.

Maybe she could stay at The Mish.

Uncle Lincoln and Aunty Pearl won't let anything happen to her.

If you can't find another place to go, even temporarily, then you'll have to stay.

You can go to court to get custody of her. Or something. Someone has to.

Play it by ear.

The Mish was already bustling as the train came into the clearing. The fires were roaring. The billies were boiling. Kids were being washed in big galvanised laundry tubs. Brooms swept everything clean. Dogs looked for scraps and laundry was hung out to dry. Those on the grog'd still be in their humpies. My loud piercing whistle and waving from the window got Uncle Lincoln's attention.

The platform seemed smaller than I remembered. Large cream silky heads of grass swayed in the slight breeze either side of me as I made my way down to the Tree of Knowledge. Uncle Lincoln, Lionel, and Ethel pulled up. They were sorry they hadn't contacted me but they hadn't wanted me to worry.

The town'd organised the dingo drive. They told me that everyone had walked in from each corner on Grandfather's old cattle property into the middle of it in an effort to flush Baby Girl out but she'd managed to avoid them.

Uncle Lincoln said Nippur, the best tracker they could find, told them that Baby Girl was walking backwards in the searchers' footprints as well as her own. She was one step ahead of them. Nippur and the others from The Mish were following her but she knew the bush as well as they did. They were leaving some tucker for her to pick up but the whole town knew she'd ridden out there initially in an attempt to kill herself. She'd sent Rebel back. When her horse had trotted into town with his saddle still on it'd chilled everyone to the bone. Rebel'd taken himself into the front yard where Dad was. He'd gone as white as a sheet they said. Mum greeted the horse and empty saddle with fury.

I wrote a note to tell Baby Girl I was back in town and to come in.

Nothing bad would happen to her. Uncle Lincoln dropped me off then he and the others went back out to where they thought Baby Girl was. I walked up the gravel path. I didn't feel as if I had the right to go into the house unannounced so I knocked on the door. I left my bag right where I could grab it if I had to make a run for it.

Mum came out to see who it was.

'Still no word.'

Then she saw Uncle Lincoln driving off.

'That's right. Draw attention to us. I hope they're having a good gossip.'

She swayed on brown high–heeled sandals down the hallway puffing on her cigarette. I followed her to the kitchen where Dad was sitting with a bottle of rum for company. He was using the poker he'd fired up in the coals in the stove to burn the sunspots off his arms. It was obvious he'd stayed at home to keep an eye on Mum. She leaned again the kitchen bench, dressed in a tartan shirtwaister with a high white collar. A neat brown patent leather belt gathered her waist together.

I rolled a cigarette and positioned myself near an exit and away from the poker.

'Those bloody things'll kill you.' Dad snapped as he got up to put the poker back in the fire.

'So will living here it seems.' I drawled as I blew the smoke out.

'I won't have you say a word about the family.'

Dad always bellowed when he was out of his depth.

'Not one bloody word. If you only come back here to cause bloody trouble then git.'

Mum giggled. Even though Baby Girl was hiding out in the bush, Mum was still the centre of attention. I looked at both of them. They no longer frightened me. After Rupert no one frightened me. I forced myself to find my voice.

'If you don't find BG somewhere else to live by tonight, Dad I'll take you to court for custody of her. If you reckon you're embarrassed now just think how you'll feel on Monday.'

Mum looked nervously at Dad.

'There's nothin' wrong with livin' here.'

As Mum went 'ing!' in the background, she turned on the radio to recite the opening to White Coolies.

'Missing,' she recited with the actors. "Missing.' She continued until she go to Vivien Bullwinkle's name. 'Here!' Mum snapped with satisfaction.

I turned from watching Mum lost in her battle as a nurse with cruel Japanese soldiers to Dad.

'You know that's not true.'

I had nothing to lose.

'You know there's something wrong with Mum. You've known for years. She takes it out on everyone but most of all she takes it out on BG.'

The words were coming out faster and louder than I intended.

'I'm not going to keep quiet about it anymore. She drove Henry away. And me. This is BG's second attempt at killing herself with others I probably don't know about. We've all had a go at killing ourselves. Don't you think that's wrong? BG's not even twelve yet. She's a good little kid. She tries so hard. Don't you think you should at least try to protect her?'

'Your mother has bad nerves. The doctor gave her some pills for them.'

Mum came out of her radio reverie.

'Besides if just one of you children were worth two bob we wouldn't be the way we are.'

I glared at Mum very hard before I turned back to Dad.

'You have to face facts. You can't spend your life hiding out in the bush pretending there's nothing wrong. You've got to find another place for BG to live today or I'm taking her back to the city with me.'

'You think you're so smart, don't you? She's still out in the bush somewhere so good luck finding her. Nippur and the others can't.'

'Well, why aren't you out looking for her, Mum? Uncle Lincoln and Lionel have gone out to get her. They know where she is. She's too scared to come home.'

I turned back to Dad.

'Is that what you want? For all of us to be terrified of you? I have to go back to the city tomorrow night so you'd better do something about it right now.'

Dad scrapped his chair back.

I quickly moved towards the exit just in case.

He picked up the keys to the ute.

I walked out to the veranda behind him.

Dad backed the ute out then turned to go up the street. Red dog hung his head out near Dad's window.

I went into Baby Girl's room, packed her things then brought them out to the front verandah. I put her small bag alongside mine. Mum slammed the front door behind me and bolted it. Dad was gone for hours. I sat on the steps waiting, hoping he wasn't up in the pub drowning his sorrows.

Hunger pangs came and went.

Late into the night Dad returned with Uncle Lincoln, Nippur and Baby Girl in the back of the ute. She didn't look much worse for the wear. I moved over protectively as Mum flung open the front door dramatically and came down the stairs.

'You absolute disgrace.'

'I've found someone to take her in.' Dad cut her off gruffly.

Jake drove up to the house, parked and got out. She used to live across the creek from us. She was very tiny with a shock of brown hair and bright blue eyes. She was always dressed in fawn coloured jodhpurs, brown riding boots and a neat white shirt. Everyone took their sick and injured animals to her. Jake and her husband taught all the kids in town how to ride at the Pony Club.

Mum flounced back into the house to avoid any more embarrassment or confrontation.

'Get in BG.' Jake offered with a warm smile. 'I'll take you home.'

I gave Baby Girl a hug. 'This is the best I can do at short notice, BG. Tell me if it doesn't work out. I'll come and get you.'

I put her bag in the boot of Jake's car.

I scribbled out my work phone number and address and gave them to Jake. 'Uncle Lincoln always knows where I am as well.'

'Good-oh.' Jake grinned as she got in the car before she drove away with Baby Girl.

Mum appeared out of the shadows.

'You've worn out your welcome here.'

'I don't think I ever had one in the first place, did I?'

I shook Dad's hand.

'Thank you. It couldn't have been easy.'

'Get in. I'll drop you near the station. We have to go out to work first light.'

I picked up my bag and got in the back of the ute near Uncle Lincoln.

As we drove up the main street every dog in the town went into a barking frenzy. Red dog gave back as good as he got.

'We've got our marching orders,' Uncle Lincoln said. 'The council have bought up all the spare houses in town. The Red Cross is going to help us move into them. We won't be at The Mish after next week.'

I took his hand and squeezed it.

The Mish was the last patch of land their mob had.

We were even going to take that off them.

'Ethel and the women are looking forward to it,' Lionel added. 'They've all been making curtains. It'll have running water as well.'

'Won't have to pay all those crooks to cart it over anymore.' Uncle

Lincoln gestured towards the taxi rank. 'Be a damned sight easier to keep clean as well. And get the kids to school.'

Dad pulled the ute up near the station.

Uncle Lincoln and Lionel hugged me.

'Thank you so much for finding BG. I'll send your mail to the Post Office.'

I shook hands with the others.

'Jake'll be real good to BG. Don't worry. You know, Jen,' Uncle Lincoln held onto my hand, 'your father's a good bloke. He does the best he can.'

I hopped out of the back of the ute. 'I know.'

I pinched myself really hard so I didn't cry.

Dad tooted the horn and drove off.

Ethel caught up to Dad in Uncle Lincoln's car. She had the rest of the mob with her. They followed Dad over to The Mish.

I walked in the semi–darkness into the station. I could sleep in the waiting room. My stomach rumbled. I realised I hadn't eaten since I left Brisbane. I looked around for water. With a lot of luck by the time the train arrived in Brisbane on Monday morning and I ran from the Roma Street Station to the office, I'd only be a few minutes late and I wouldn't lose my job.

As I wrapped myself up on the railway seat, I dialled my radio around to find someone to keep me company.

As Patsy Cline began to sing The Tennessee Waltz, a terrible sadness and longing told me I'd probably never see the town or come back home again. I couldn't come back home again.

I sobbed in silence while I sat under the stars and waited for the train.

ROLLIN' DOWN THE ROAD

Rupert's arms came through the window and locked around my throat. Childhood habits had kept my legs just out from under the bedclothes. The nuns used to beat us if we didn't sleep the right way. I put my feet on the edge of the window trying with all my might to shut it on him. Finally he had to let go.

The Italian woman rang the police despite my protests not to. She pointed out the strangulation marks around my throat. The police told her unless he attacked me on the street in broad daylight they couldn't do anything about him or help me. It was a domestic situation. They never interfered in domestic situations.

71

'That one.' The Italian woman summed Rupert up. 'He think he a gift from God. Our lord saviour Jesus Christ was the first to say he was a gift from God.' She blessed herself. 'Now they're all gifts from God one way or the other. Can't take no for an answer.'

Rupert was outside the office as I left work. Smiling. Charming. While I froze he put his arm around me as if he were a boyfriend, delighted to see me again. He squeezed me tightly as he shoved me into a corner of the Renoir cafe.

Amid the luxurious leather chairs, rich warm autumn colours, lavish lamps, Renoir's plump paintings, chocolate cakes and creamed deserts, Rupert told me that now we were together again we could discuss life, love, politics and where we were going with our relationship. He told me he'd worked out a gambling system to win millions on horses. His smile lit up his face as he ordered coffee from the waitress. He also needed money to get started with the bookies and he knew I'd have enough to get him started.

I sat in silence with screams that couldn't get out. He wanted sex— brutal shoved in the alley sex. And more money. He wanted me to meet his mother—a broken down woman with broken teeth. Rupert loved her but in the same hateful way he told me he loved me.

Almost instantly I fell back into using the skills I'd learned in the convent and my family. Obedience. It didn't matter what anyone did to my body they'd never get me. I'd survived them. I'd survive this.

After a few weeks I overcame a lifetime of training from Dad and I went to the police. Even though I couldn't tell them Rupert's surname, address or anything much about him, they acted as my complaint of rape and attempted murder was a lover's tiff.

'He doesn't seem like the sort of bloke that'd have to do that to get a woman, luv.'

The coppers smiled as they escorted me from the premises.

'You women do nothing but whinge at the drop of a hat over nothing. If every woman who got a bit of a love tap wanted protection from the police, we wouldn't have enough coppers to go round. We'd all be in jail if you had your way.'

Rupert grabbed me as I stood at the traffic lights outside the Police Station. He began to swing me out into the on–coming traffic, over and over, pulling me back just before a car or a truck hit me.

I can't breathe.

I can't breathe.

'See? I can do anything I like to you. I can kill you if I want to. No one cares. You'll never get away from me. Never. No one is ever going to help you or believe you. No one'd even look for you.'

The passers–by stood beside me as they waited to cross at the lights. They could see what was happening but they walked on. Rupert eventually let me go and disappeared into the darkness. I never knew when he was going to strike. On one occasion when he threw me out in front of a truck it grazed my face.

I checked with Jake to see if Baby Girl was alright. She said she was then she told me everyone from The Mish was now living in the town. It was providing a rough and ready protection for everyone.

It was time for me to go.

When I opened the door at the doss-house Rupert was lying on the bed flipping through my bankbook. The window was open.

'I've had a great idea. You can keep me while I go to University to get my degree.'

His smile never reaches his eyes.

'Then I'll keep you so you can get yours. You told me you wanted to go to Uni. We have to make arrangements to get married soon too.'

I don't know your last name.

'I said I'd make an honest woman out of you.'

I have plans for my own life.

'I'll pick you up at lunchtime tomorrow and we can turn your bank account into a joint one.'

He handed my book back to me.

'You'd better go.' I stuttered as I tried to string a sentence together. 'I'll get into trouble from the landlady if she sees you here. I'm not allowed have men in my room.'

He got off the bed. He gave me a long lingering kiss before he walked off into the night. Swallowing vomit I locked the window, shoved the bed up against the door and then sat on it. I put my bankbook in my purse along with anything I had of value.

In the morning the Italian woman looked a little startled as I left my room and handed her back the key. I went to shake her hand but she grabbed me and kissed me on both cheeks. I was dressed in all the clothes I possessed, one outfit over the top of the other and my transistor radio shoved down the front. I figured Rupert was probably watching me, hopefully from a distance.

I walked through the front door of the office, smiled and waved a good morning to everyone before I went out the back door, ran out onto the street and caught the first bus that came past. I slid down in the seat until it'd made it to the next suburb. I got on and off buses for several hours each time carefully checking that Rupert hadn't followed me. Near sunset I reached the outskirts of Brisbane as a goods train slowed to go around a bend.

As I ran alongside it, fellow travellers put out their hands to help me swing up onto it.

The city disappeared as we swept through the bush. By morning we'd reached the edge of Sydney. Dog tired I jumped off the train and made my way to the suburban stations.

Purple–blue jacaranda petals and half–eaten mulberries lay thickly on the springtime footpaths. Possums had moved swiftly through the dark to remove the best ripe fruit before anyone else got a chance. Bush tucker was everywhere.

A room in a Glebe boarding house had given me shelter.

A team of solicitors in Macquarie Street'd employed me to work as a typist in their office. I'd past their spelling and typing test and I was well-spoken enough to answer the telephones.

On my way home from work I'd followed the familiar toasty smell of rice to the BBQ King in Goulburn Street. Dozens of red lacquered ducks and slabs of shiny barbequed pork were hung in its front window.

'Hello Ladies and Gentleman.'

The cheery owner put down the racing guide to show me to a seat before he went back behind the cash register. The races galloped loudly from the radio as a waiter hovered for my order.

Duck and rice with pickled vegetables and some chrysanthemum tea was put on the table. I read the papers left behind by the lunchtime crowds. If I was feeling wealthy I ate twice a day.

Afterwards I walked around the streets looking in windows, watching people buzz around with trolleys filled with boxes of fruit and vegetables while others had sides of beef or pork on their shoulders.

I broadened my taste buds by eating stuff on sticks with a sauce that blistered my tongue at the Malaya. I'd entered a whole new world of smell and taste as I slowly began to make my way through different Asian countries.

Sydney was made up of all sorts from everywhere much the same as the town had been. It was multi-coloured like a medieval city from long ago. Occasionally, as the bats swarmed through the night sky, well–fed foxes make a run for it across a road. Their daring–do made me smile. During the day snakes took a nervous chance of lying in a patch of sun so they could get going for the day. They knew city people didn't expect them to be in their streets so they remained visibly invisible—ratting to earn their keep.

When I'd first arrived the landlady asked me where my luggage was. I told her I was wearing it but I could pay her cash to rent the room for the week. She looked me over for a few seconds. "Fair enough," she'd replied. She got out some keys and handed me a set.

We walked upstairs to a spic and Spartan room. A shared bathroom was down the corridor. Some bath towels were in the cupboard and she changed the sheets once a week. A coin-operated laundry was out the back. I handed over the rent and locked the door. I pulled the radio out of my pocket, put it on the side table then turned it on to see what Sydney sounded like. Australians trying to mimic being British or American.

From my handbag I got out toothbrush and paste. As I took all my clothes off except for the initial layer I put them in the cupboard. After showering I selected clean jeans and a t–shirt. I lay on the bed to think about what I was going to do next. Sydney, it seemed was full of love songs too. My heart nearly leapt out of my chest when someone knocked on the door. The landlady spoke through it. She wanted to talk to me for a minute. Two men stood alongside her. They held large canvas laundry bags.

'I don't want to bother you, dear,' the landlady said, 'but, not that we ask why around here, but we thought you might need some more clothes.'

'We saw you on the way in.'

The first stocky man looked me up and down, measuring me with his eyes.

'Figured you were about a ten or a twelve.'

The other man was covered in tattoos.

'Yair. You look like you could do with a good feed.'

They smiled.

Mum always bought me size eighteen or twenty.

I frowned at the men in front of me.

'We brought these around for you to try on. They're the latest fashions from Paris. All the underthings you girls wear match and stuff. We'll leave them with you. Just pick out what you want and give us the bag back when you have finished with it.'

'They work on the wharves, dear.'

The landlady thought it was enough explanation. I had no idea what that meant.

'I don't have much money.'

'Pay us when you've got it,' the short man coughed. 'They fell off the back of a truck. They're salvage, so to speak.'

As they smiled in unison, they looked like every rogue relative my family or the town had ever produced.

Within the hour I was dressed in Chanel, Dior, Westwood and other designers I'd never heard of. I had matching lacy bras and underpants for each outfit. The wharfies gave me different coloured packets of Gitanes to smoke so they matched my outfits.

The next morning I went to look for a job in my new finery stopping only to buy a pair of serviceable shoes to go with everything. I started my new job with the solicitors the following Monday and paid the wharfies back with my first pay packet.

As the days passed I realised I had to give some more of my life away in order to survive. I cancelled the correspondence lessons I'd started in the hope of going to university. The teacher wrote back to ask me to reconsider as I was doing extremely well. I couldn't think of what to say to him.

With my piano playing long gone because I had nowhere to practice or the hours needed in order to do it properly, all I had left of my original ambition was writing. It was portable and could be packed up quickly if necessary. I didn't need space or an address. I bought a notebook and some pens. I found an old black second–hand typewriter in a pawnshop.

I organised my life to rotate around work to keep a roof over my head, experimenting with Asian food in the cheap cafes I'd found, the radio and writing. I saved money on a ribbon by not using the typewriter until I had something truly memorable to type.

I began to work my way up at the job with my wages increasing a tiny bit at a time. I still couldn't afford a place of my own. I wouldn't be able to until after I turned twenty–one and earned an adult female wage. It was still only a bit more than half the male wage but I was getting tantalising closer to breathing clear air.

I knew that once a woman got married she was usually forced to leave her job and become dependent on a man for everything she needed. In return she was expected to please him in every way. Divorce was almost impossible to get. Far too many men thought they could treat a woman any which way they wanted because she had no choice but to put up with it, if she wanted to keep a roof over her head. Marriage ended women's lives in more ways than one.

The message was clear—never tell anyone anything about yourself.

Wherever I went men made gross sexual suggestions and passes at me. I thought it was because they'd figured out I was 'damaged goods' as Mum used to call women who had sex without the benefit of marriage. I'd finally understood what she was talking about.

I wondered what happened if you were a damaged good and got married. Did it somehow undo the damage? Did you become a good good again? Did damaged goods get married? Or have relationships with other men or could you only have sex with the first man you had sex with?

I simply didn't know and there was no one I could ask. I didn't want to feel any more stupid than I already did.

I was always very careful never to be alone with men or within touching distance. Even then some would manage to grab my breasts or my behind. I avoided public transport because there they could blame rough driving for the fact they rubbed up against me. "Are you on the pill?" they'd ask undaunted by the fact I'd never seen them before. "Well give us a fuck then."

Men loved the way The Pill meant women could have sex without becoming pregnant. They'd calculated far quicker than women had that it did not bode well for them in the future. If women could control their own bodies then they'd be able to control their own lives. So they demanded women still have a 'period' each month so they'd remain 'natural' and less of a threat. It was completely unnecessary. Women still checked the back of their dresses five days out of every month. They could never get away from the reality of their biology. Like the exaggerated erect church spires they'd designed, men had to be reassured about their dominance at all times. Each time a man came near me my heart would twist and I couldn't breathe; struck dumb. No matter how much of a talking to I gave myself I couldn't stop it.

I rang Jake's place to give her my new address. Baby Girl was going to continue in high school until she got her leaving certificate. She told me Dad'd bought a hotel near Brisbane.

He was enjoying being a publican. The clientele came from the nearby Air Force Base and each night there was a fistfight.

Jake told me that Mum'd call out, "Tom! Tom!" to demand he come back to the bar before she'd hide out in the lounge room to pretend she wasn't related to him. It was several fights in, Jake chuckled, before Mum leaned over the bar to see it was Dad wrestling on the floor with someone in uniform. He remained undefeated.

Mum hated the whole idea of running a hotel. She still refused to work but she did tend the counter if necessary. She had many rules around what made up 'necessary'. When she thought she recognised anyone coming into the hotel she'd crouch behind the bar until they left.

The bar patrons had taken to calling her 'Madge the Mystery Barmaid'.

She'd taken up playing the piano to drown out the sound of Dad's biffing everyone but she soon found herself surrounded by drunken patrons singing along. Hang out your washing on the Siegfried Line was a favourite among the military. Despite herself she'd become a huge hit and the crowds increased.

Dad'd bought the pub as a retirement option he could run on his own but now he had to ask Henry to come in to help him because the patrons were spilling out onto the footpath.

Henry didn't harbor a grudge and took up bar work, initially just on the weekends. He was very good at it.

It seemed everyone had set themselves up in one way or another. Life might've been rougher than guts but it was workable. I briefly thought about going up to see them but then thought twice. I wasn't twenty–one yet and I didn't trust them. And besides, was I the only one to think it wasn't a good idea for the family to be involved with running a pub?

One morning while I walked to work the air tried to block my way. My body carefully noted everything happening around me. My brain was on high alert. A quick cold wind blew down the street. It whirled around me then left. Goosebumps shivered up and down my back and neck then into my arms.

I began to run from building to building. When I arrived at work the manager beckoned me to come over. My stomach began to flutter and my heart twisted in fear. We walked towards his office.

'We've employed a new man to take over from Lachlan.'

As he pushed the door open, Rupert stood up to greet me.

I backed into the manager to get away.

He pushed me slightly forward to get me off his foot.

'Jenny, I'd like you to meet Rupert Howard. Rupert, this is Jenny Jae.'

Rupert extended his hand to shake mine. He crushed it. The pain took my breath away. I thought he'd broken every bone in it.

'Jenny will show you around the office, Rupert. Welcome aboard.'

Rupert gave the manager a handsome dazzling smile.

I can't breathe.

I can't breathe.

I walked out of the office with Rupert.

'So how's Glebe? Do they have a spare room there or shall we share yours?'

Rupert lowered his voice so the rest of the office couldn't hear.

'I thought we could celebrate our reunion at that café you like.'

Just before we came up to the reception desk he added some more menace to his information.

'I'm going to really enjoy getting to know all your colleagues as well. I've been watching them too.'

My body split into pieces. One part was going through the motions—one felt sick and swallowed gulps of vomit—the other began to do a stock take.

Your bankbook is in your handbag.

Rupert was being charming and witty. No one would believe me.

You've got a week's worth of cash in your purse.
With each staff introduction he snuffed the life out of me.
Your room only has stuff in it.
Rupert never let me out of his sight.
It's only stuff.
The clock edged towards five.
There has to be a train going somewhere tonight. Or a truck if I can get to the highway.
As I moved around the office, Rupert's eyes never left me. I had to get out of the building.
Lie doggo.
I slipped a razor sharp silver letter opener into my handbag.
Don't panic. Don't panic.
The building'll get me out me out safely.
Rupert towered over me.
'Time to go.'
Gravel, dirt and ash.
I picked up my handbag.
'I need to go to the ladies. Freshen up.'
He hesitated but just then one of the office girls distracted him. As they chatted I went down the corridor towards the lavatories.
I took my shoes off, pushed the fire stairs door open quietly then ran down fifteen flights. Out on the street I hailed a taxi.
'Central Station.'
I bought a ticket to Melbourne. I hid in the women's lavatory watching the platform. When the train was just about to pull out I jumped into it. I stood inside the doorway to check the platforms as we departed. Rupert wasn't there. I stayed awake all night keeping vigil. After I got to Melbourne I hitchhiked back up to Brisbane. It took days to travel thousands of miles.

The boarding house in Upper Edward Street had a vacancy.
The owner gave me a job so I could pay the rent. As well as cleaning I helped cook breakfasts, washed up, made beds and dusted Hans Heysen paintings. On every wall luminous golden, grey, pink, and blue gum trees were framed into their large landscapes. The owner didn't believe in putting money in the bank.

The tenants were dancers and singers from the various musicals touring the country. They reminded me of The Fairy Man I'd met years ago.
And Henry.
They had an air of wildness about them that came from being an outsider. Self–sufficient they had a witty comeback to any slurred

remarks as they sang and danced their way through life. Strong, supple, street–wise and mouthy, they and their mob could biff with the best of them if they had to. It seemed to be as frequently as Dad.

I was exhausted from being on the run. I needed a place of my own. I wanted to make friends, have a worthwhile job and talk about politics, literature and life with people over a nicely cooked homemade meal. Writing was getting further and further away from me too as was any hope of trying to do something with my life. Or even be allowed to have one. It seemed I was destined to be a cleaner. I tried to keep hope alive by putting a few words into the notepad I kept in my purse.

It took Rupert a few months to find me but by the time he did, I had someone bigger, stronger and smarter than he was.

In fact all the boys from *My Fair Lady* were on my side and they were waiting for him. He couldn't get to me and as suddenly as he appeared he left.

After the show closed the boys and I moved on to Sydney.

MODIGLIANI

Bob Dylan wailed on his harmonica as the party in our shared inner–city house kicked up a notch and was now in full swing.

Some of us were dressed in short miniskirts with long knee-high dark brown Spanish leather boots. Others wore black pants topped with a black polo–necked skivvy. Neon yellow, orange, and strawberry pink beads swung around our necks, massed bangles clattered on our wrists, and chandelier earrings flowed around our ears. Beehive and bouffant hair was teased into place. Curls fell down our cheeks.

Guys mooched around in denim jeans, paisley shirts, beards, long hair, and wooden beads trying to appear artistic or at least musically inclined. Mostly they were looking for a free feed, money, sex and someone to wait on them or all of it at the same time. Bob Dylan with his rudimentary singing and uneasy elevation as the saviour of social causes inspired their poetical and musical ambitions. However most of them didn't seem all that interested in doing much about injustice or holding down a job. Men liked me because I paid my own way and if they hung around long enough, theirs as well.

With my housemates, Nancy, Kitty, and Trisha, we'd put together a substantial spread—small quiches minus bacon for the vegetarians; fondue centered on the table while long-stemmed dipping forks resting alongside small squares of toasted bread; slices of black pumpernickel lay in temptation near the cream cheese while Frank Zappa started to sing a song about it on our record player. Thin slices of smoked salmon curled up around the ice while fronds of dill rested in a small glass pot nearby. Cheddar cheese pieces weaved around slices of bright green and crisp white Granny Smith apples. We honoured Tom Wolfe's *The Electric Kool–Aid Acid Test* with frosty pitchers of the green and orange powdered drink minus the acid.

We'd laughed as we'd set up the table that while we believed in the right to choose the Menzies' cohort—the church, unions and others too terrified to move with the times—vehemently opposed a woman having a choice about anything.

'Barry Goldwater is my man,' Ron, the American exchange student said. 'He's got my vote.'

My housemates eyebrows raised.

I'd met them at the hospital up the road where we worked as glorified cleaners. They were looking for someone to take over a spare room and I had just arrived from Brisbane in search of shelter. My belongings consisted of a mattress on the floor, a battered suitcase that acted as a wardrobe, an incense burner and small notebooks filled with writing. It could be packed quickly or left behind.

Ray Charles, Aretha Franklin, Percy Sledge, Leadbelly, Howlin' Wolf and the Four Tops mingled with Dylan, Frank Zappa, the blues, soul, gospel and folk music. We didn't listen much to The Beatles or The Rolling Stones. We preferred the original black blues and gospel sound to the one filtered through white people.

I read HD's Bid me to Live and flipped through the pop magazine *Go–Set*. Some nights we'd dance wildly to Zorba the Greek in the rain and on others tried to find our feet.

I'd saved up enough money to buy myself black and white flowered designer clothes from Prue Acton as fanfare for my twenty–first birthday.

The party conversation had turned into an argument about the American War in Vietnam. In the mid-nineteen fifties America'd appealed to Menzies' vanity by asking him to be an ally in it.

The Americans had trained and armed Ho Chi Minh, the Vietnamese nationalist leader, to help fight the Japanese during the Second World War. Ho was on Australia's side when it needed every ally it could get after its abandonment by Britain.

After the war, when Ho declared he wanted independence for his country, the Americans called him a communist and turned on him to side with the French. The French and their Catholic cronies didn't want to leave Vietnam. It gave them status especially after they'd lost most of it because of their behaviour in the Second World War.

Menzies, they reasoned could easily manage a small war provided he had considerable help. The Second World War was obviously out of his league. The Labor Party had to take it over.

America decided to put the boot into Vietnam by sending its poor and its people of colour to carry it out. At first to soften the population up Menzies only sent in advisors. It allowed him to strut up and down the country as a wartime leader fighting the good fight against communism. Now he and his cohort under Malcolm Fraser'd brought in conscription by birthday ballot. Another day of celebration became a grim occasion.

'Wasn't it Goldwater that said Vietnam was as big as most major European nations?' I asked Ron. 'I think its history goes back to 111BC or thereabouts.'

'Dunno,' Ron replied. 'If it's good for America then it's good enough for me."

'Don't you care about going into a war with a country you don't know anything about?'

'Australia goes into everything with considerable ignorance,' Irene replied. 'Menzies is a know all who knows nothing.'

'We call him Winston Churchill Jnr.,' Kitty said.

'Only because he's the same size as the original,' Irene added.

'I thought your preachers in America were taking the Republican Party over to make it into a religious organisation.'

Ben, our Canadian friend loved tormenting Ron and his right-wing views.

'Oh ha ha,' Ron replied.

'He did say homosexuals have a right to be homosexuals,' Irene said.

'What about women?' I asked.

'You women always make everything about women,' Ron replied.

'In your guts you know he's nuts,' Ben whispered so Ron could overhear.

'In your heart you know he's right,' Ron replied.

'That's true,' Ben replied. 'Really, really right … wing.'

They kept squabbling.

Feminism had nudged a few men into saying they supported our claim for equality but there was nothing they could do except to keep benefitting themselves under the current arrangement. There was an underlying malice in their behaviour. It manifested itself in vicious gossip, rudeness, bullying, as well as physical, sexual and vitriolic verbal abuse, threats, violence, cutting us out of the conversation and white–anting women out of work and wages. It didn't take long to work out that most men simply didn't care about conditions for women.

Our protest zap actions such as throwing boa–constrictor corsets, pancake cosmetics, hats, scarves and gloves into the rubbish bin was breathlessly reported as 'bra burning' by the media. Although women hadn't burnt their bras the newspapers insisted we would've if we thought of it as they had because we'd gone mad with militant feminism. Occasionally men would grab our legs and run their hands up and down them and say, "Oh thank god you're still shaving."

Through loud guffaws and 'hear hears' our parliamentary representatives felt moved to comment that without bras Australian women'd end up looking like the natives in the National Geographic magazines. They'd also told us we'd failed our biological reality by following feminism. Still, most women around me were trying to choose partners they hoped they could change or at least last the distance from a pool of men who weren't interested in redefining their relationships with them at all.

Australia wouldn't even redefine itself let alone have a conversation about who we were now and where we wanted to go. Even with our world–class inventions and achievements Australia still distrusted and discounted anything that was Australian because it couldn't, by virtue of being Australian, be any good or have any value. It suited the beneficiaries of these beliefs to keep inserting shame into the Australian psyche about its white convict and colonial beginnings to continue to rob us of anything that might make us a quid.

We had long arguments about why the Australian male was the Australian male and generally agreed that by seventeen hundreds slavery had begun to be frowned upon as uncivilized so Britain got around it by sentencing their convicts to seven years transportation to Australia for a trifling crime. Seven years was enough time for the convicts to set up a British colony for nothing more than the occasional meal and a good flogging. The Scots among them established banking, farming and philosophy; the Irish contributed the political fevour; the Cornish made bricks; the Welsh mined; and the English designed the architecture and made laws that enshrined their pickpocketing behaviour and white upper class supremacy.

Convict women also had the added sexual responsibility of stopping 'unnatural crimes' among the male convicts. This was in addition to working all day for an overlord then coming home to cook, wash, mind children and clean—by candlelight and a few coals.

The Australian male never evolved much from the seventeen hundreds. He still believed that just as female convicts'd finished their daily backbreaking labour and household duties for their owners, we should continue doing it for him today.

Britain was still looting us a hundred and fifty years later. Glimpses of the royal family and knighthoods rewarded those who kept the population in its place—as a third rate European.

Back in the beginning it didn't take long for the first–born children of the convicts to note Aborigines had a group of elders that governed through a socially responsible, democratic decision–making process. They also had a pretty good lifestyle when compared to the penal colony. The first–borns were free and owed Britain nothing. Without much fanfare some of them walked out to join the blackfellas in the bush to farm, share knowledge and weaponry. Those who remained in the cities were too terrified of the alien Outback to join them.

When their European magic and gods failed them and their crops, they relied on handouts, protection and patronage from Britain. It now acted as a substitute for the gods of old. In order to stay safe they became expert in acquiescence—people so desperate to avoid judgement and punishment they'd believe and do anything they were told. With one crack of the upper–class whip most Australians'd fall into a panicked mob that bellowed in fearful unison all the way to the fate imposed on them by the Mother Country.

At the same time Australians viewed themselves as outlaws that always gave authority the finger. They settled for making heroes out of the few who actually did. In return America and Britain agreed to keep Australians 'safe' by finding enough threats to keep them on edge and obsequious. Most Australians ended up on the lookout to either Britain or America to provide approval for everything they did so they could keep pretending they were something they weren't and continue to speak of it in fake plummy British accents. An Australian accent was met with disapproval and derision.

'Who said a man who stands for nothing will fall for anything?' Jim asked in order to score another point on Ron.

'Malcolm X,' I replied absently.

Dad was fond of pointing out that if you could convince the lowest whitefella that he was better than the best blackfella you could get him to agree to anything even if it was against his own best interest.

While the rest of the western world was creating wealth through education and innovation, White Australia was stagnant. Menzies was the only ruler most people had ever known, despite the fact he spent most of his time in Britain trying to get into their parliament and be 'British to his bootstraps'.

"Not that the Empire'd ever give us a hand," Uncle Lincoln and Uncle Rhodie had told us.

"Flamin' windbag," Dad'd grunted as he plastered iodine on the cuts he'd stitched up with needle and thread. The burrs in the wool could cut a shearer's hands to pieces. "All that bloke does is scare the bejesus out of the stupid. And god knows there's enough of them around."

Menzies, thwarted in his ambition to be the Prime Minister of Great Britain, continued his condescension towards his fellow Australians with as many insults he could devise just to show his constituents exactly what he thought of them.

During an acute housing shortage that saw many destitute families living in tin sheds or tents, a constituent called out to Menzies during a political rally, "'ere - what are you going to do about 'ousing?" Menzies'd held his nose. "I'm going to put an H in front of it," he'd sneered to the desperate, dispossessed and homeless.

To make everyone feel less threatened by modernity the Australian Labor Party and the Liberal Party brought in as many of our former enemies from Nazi Europe as it could. They called them the Beautiful Balts to make them seem more palatable. They were told to populate the country or Australia would perish by Yellow Peril. And communism. They passed on their politics to their children as they made themselves at home. Every one of their votes went to Menzies.

In 1956 when Egypt's President Nasser nationalised the Suez Canal the collective colonialism of Britain, France, America and Australia saw an opportunity to wave a superior stick around those it thought less white than themselves. Menzies blundered into the middle of it. He underestimated the Arab leaders just as he had Hitler.

Meanwhile his government in Australia was disagreeing whole–heartedly with him. Most thought Nasser had every right to take the Canal and the best thing to do was make sure everyone got a good deal out of it. Menzies patronising attitude towards the Arabic world infuriated everyone in it. "These Gyppos are a dangerous lot of backward adolescents, mouthing the slogans of democracy, full of self-importance and basic ignorance," Menzies wrote in his diary. He seemed completely oblivious to the fact that he could have well been describing himself and his ignorance about any subject outside the monarchy.

Menzies foray onto the world–stage was once more not only a national embarrassment but also a monumental failure. Nasser thumbed his nose at Menzies and he was soon given the bum's rush back to Australia. His determination to be a wartime leader by hook or by crook was thwarted at every turn by darkish foreign ingrates who lacked his superior breeding and intelligence.

After the debacle over the Suez Canal, Menzies needed to be seen as a player outside Australia's narrow confines to keep up appearances, America was on a communist witch-hunt and Britain needed to sell its armaments. All their agendas and ambitions now centered on one country that hadn't done anything to anybody—Vietnam.

Despite the war conducted by Aborigines since white settlement and continuing in one way or another to the present day, Menzies believed he could conquer Vietnam as he had the blackfellas, despite all evidence to the contrary. To get Australians on side so they'd invade a country that posed no threat to it, Menzies manipulated the spectre of convict ships, the blackfellas fear of invasion and conquest, and the country's violent beginnings to get what he wanted. These once–upon–a–time race and class stories were now set like cement in the fragile and frightened Australian psyche. All Menzies had to do was yank the ancient convict chain to set it all in motion.

'What's Menzies motto?' Ron asked.

'First among Equals,' I replied.

'Who thought that up?'

'George Orwell.'

For a second Ron believed me.

'Fun-nee,' he said.

However, as Menzies paraded around the war zones saluting soldiers, he didn't so much represent a great leader as more an elderly, overstuffed sock puppet on the end of British–American arm.

Aborigines, with the proud history of the military service marched off to fight Menzies' war.

While they were fighting in Vietnam on behalf of Australia, Queensland introduced a law that stated an 'assisted Aborigine' could be detained for up to a year for behaving in an 'offensive, threatening, insolent, insulting, disorderly, obscene or indecent manner' or 'leaving, escaping or attempting to leave or escape from the reserve'. Those who refused to be 'assisted' ended up in a prison called Palm Island. Despite Menzies' exceptional short sightedness and indifferent, ineffectual political and racist policies Australia continued to think of itself as a land of potential prosperity and promise.

Few Australians had taken the time to read Donald Horne's book let alone remember the full quote from it—Australia is a lucky country, run by second-rate people who share its luck—before they began to misuse it by shortening it to the lucky country. The lucky country remained at odds with its other fervent belief that it remained ever under threat from yellow hordes and others of dark ilk and intention who also wanted to share in its luck.

It seemed that whatever decent Australian folk worked for and held dear—freedom, family, and stability—it could be dashed from their grasp at any moment because of the ever-present threat from some form of atheistic, communist or jealous coloured horde, usually arriving by boat—just as Australia's swept–under–the–carpet convict forebears had.

Australians continued to fervently believe the conservative propaganda that promised one day, someday, they'd be safe and rich, with no coloureds mixed up with the whites in a carefully sorted out Monday–morning wash.

According to the popular press, its allied media and all Australian political parties, sinister, serpentine shadows lurked evilly and enviously, watching and waiting for the slightest signs of weakness in the Australian character. The dangers were everywhere, within and without. At this very moment those causing impending peril to the Australian way of life were the youth, migrants, queue jumpers, coloureds, boongs, unionists, perverts, feminists, commies, students, anti–war demonstrators, atheists, agitators, and of course, queers. They were being hunted down and destroyed in law 'n order drives, conducted by the most corrupt police force in the country.

My reveries were interrupted by my old friend, Philippe who had just arrived with half the queers in Sydney. He was almost out of breath as if he'd just ran a marathon.

'Bonsoir,' I said as Philippe kissed me on both cheeks. 'Why are you panting?'

'It's that Bumper Farrell. 'e must know every goat track in Sydney.'

'Peanuting again was he?'

Irene bought him over a glass of wine.

Peanuting was like shooting fish in a barrel for the coppers, led by Sergeant Bumper Farrell, the most corrupt bullyman in Australia. The regular arrests of homosexuals satisfied the prurient interests of the bored, drugged–up or drunken suburban housewife, the ambitious politician and the closeted gay clergy. Someone was doing something about law and order to protect Australians against their fellow Australians while corruption and crime ran rampant.

Philippe began to cruise around the room. He was a very tall, incredibly handsome, muscular, athletic and upfront homosexual.

He'd come to Australia with his tiny chic Parisian mother, Odette, through a variety of countries I didn't enquire into too deeply. Odette and Philippe adored each other. They stuck like glue but never got in each other's way or lives. It worried Odette that her son devoured men the way some consumed tea and cigarettes. Philippe's physique and charm kept him out of trouble most days; his fists on others. I'd met him and his long suffering boyfriend, John through my all–dancing, all–singing *My Fair Lady* protection squad.

Our party was in full swing when, uninvited, the French Navy turned up. Philippe was in his element. As some sailors moved into the kitchen to get more food and proposition women, others went with Philippe to the nearest bedroom.

Philippe's boyfriend John, half–crazy from a jealousy that threatened to suffocate him, turned up. He refused to have any of the punch or food I offered as a decoy. He started calling out for Philippe, demanding to know where he was. He saw a French sailor sneaking out of the bedroom followed by several more. John dramatically threw open the bedroom door.

'You slllluuuuuttt,' he hissed.

Philippe boomed back in his singsong voice.

'I am not a slut. I am just very popular. Anyway, 'ow dare you check up on me?'

'Keep your voice down.'

'Which one of youse blokes painted this nude sheila blue?'

The Bullymen had muscled their way into the lounge room. We were so caught up in Philippe and John's drama we hadn't heard the police arrive.

'Yeeeharrr,' someone screamed in the background. Another sucked on a joint then passed it on. They hadn't notice the coppers were there either. Bob Dylan continued to thump out from every loud speaker.

'Which one of youse painted this nude sheila?'

The Bullymen were getting impatient.

The candles blinked when the lights came on.

Most of us were folded into purple velvet cushions and chocolate beanbags. Incense burned the room blue. I noticed the women were at one end of the room and the men were at the other.

'Come on.'

They were getting louder.

'Which one of youse did this?'

They flourished a poster they'd ripped off the wall.

'Modigliani.'

I signalled Kitty to warn Philippe and John.

The Bullymen had another look at the print of the painting then at us.

'Which one of youse is him?'

Someone laughed unkindly but got a swift kick to shut them up.

'I thought I saw him in the kitchen.'

Nancy looked very intellectual with her thick black rimmed glasses and short curly hair.

Trisha went to stand beside Don just in case. She was more concerned about getting him to marry her than making a stand.

'He was out in the kitchen a few minutes ago,' Ben added.

Butter wouldn't melt in their mouths.

'What's he look like?' the cops asked.

'Um, you know, like most Italians. Like a dago.' I struggled out of the beanbag. 'Um he's kind of short, dark, smells of garlic, has a funny accent, wears a lime green suit. That's right isn't it, Nancy?'

After the police tramped into the kitchen most of the party shot through.

The rest of us helped the police in their search for the wanted painter.

'Modigliani. Come on out. The police want to speak to you. Yoo-hoo. Where are you? Modigliani.'

The French Navy had frowns on their faces.

'Why do you want Modigliani? He dead.'

Nancy and Kitty were trying to mime with various gestures for them to be quiet.

'Gee that's funny,' I told the police. 'He was here.'

We went back to the lounge room. Philippe and John were holding hands with Kitty and Nancy. Philippe began kissing Kitty's hand as if completely enamoured. John shot him a furious look but then decided to out–amour him. One copper looked at the golden Klimt kiss poster I had on the wall. He took it down, rolled it up and tucked it under his arm.

'Youse lot lay off the booze and call it a night.'

The copper walked out with his companions. He didn't give any explanation about why he took Klimt or Modigliani with him.

There was one lone bottle of beer, a huge amount of chocolate and half dozen people left who could hardly stand up without giggling.

Sam Cooke sexed down the hallway and we began to twist the night away while Sam sang.

'Zieg Heil!'

We put our arms up in mock salute as we danced.

We partied most nights and worked or marched away our days in the hope we could make a difference and change the government as well as our lives.

I wondered more and more whether I should stay in it or go abroad like everyone else and see if I could make it there.

Ever under threat by the Australian establishment for being different or non-conformist as they called it, we knew what fun we had wouldn't last, so we made the most of it while we could.

HENRY

Henry had met a small raw–boned woman with a scrawny voice called Amanda Reith.

Tanned, whippet–thin with a blonde beehive, designer clothes and long pink fingernails Amanda had wriggled her way into the family. She had been engaged to marry a grazier from the Western Downs, but he'd dumped her at the last minute. Everyone reckoned his parents could see 'access to family trust fund' written all over Amanda's face even though she denied any interest in money whatsoever. After they'd vetoed the wedding Amanda'd turned her attention to Henry almost immediately. It was a screw you to her former fiancée and his family. She could get anyone she wanted just by clicking her fingers.

I don't think Henry knew what hit him or even if he thought it mightn't be wise to marry someone within a few weeks of meeting them in a bar.

'Henry,' I began. 'I don't know Amanda but I do know you. You shouldn't be getting married.'

Henry turned on me.

'Don't tell me what to do.'

As he began to walk away, he muttered, 'It'll cure me.'

I called after him.

'That's not true. There's no cure.'

Amanda had already moved in. Henry'd told Dad she'd make herself useful around the hotel but as Dad pointed out, she was hardly out of bed before midday so her usefulness was somewhat limited. Mum told me she couldn't stand Amanda but as she was probably all that Henry'd get, she couldn't look a gift horse in the mouth. Mum and Amanda had a few things in common as far as I could see—smoking, drinking tea and keeping up appearances. They were both very thin.

Dad struggled to be civil to Amanda's parents while Mum made it plain they were beneath her. Reg and Rae were born–again Christians of a Lutheran kind. Amanda was their only child. To supplement his stipend, their Preacher, a blow–in from New Zealand, clear–felled land with a heavy chain strung between two tractors that destroyed everything in its path. It was a cheap and quick. The Preacher stood for everything Dad was against. He'd used the pulpit and the bible to campaign for a seat in Parliament. Now he was running the State. Reg and Rae thought he was the greatest man who ever lived. The Preacher'd brought his cheap and quick chainsaw philosophy into the Parliament, the State, and then later tried to spread it throughout the rest of the country. There was no more red tape. Provided they had money in a brown paper bag or similar, everyone could do whatever they liked without unions, do–gooders, commies, the police or anyone else poking their noses in.

'You know Bob Menzies was very fond of people who were in various German Christian Socialist Parties,' Dad began by way of conversation when Reg and Rae dropped in for a drink before they picked up their daughter. 'Especially in the nineteen thirties. Didn't the Preacher invite them over here to have a bit of a squint at us then, Rene? So they could see what they too could get out of us when they got here. They had a big influence on him.'

'Is that a fact?' Reg nodded his head wisely.

He didn't know what Dad was talking about but he collected the information anyway. He probably could and would use it later to sound important as if he'd had a brainwave all by himself.

Reg was a puffed up little man who thought he knew everything and everybody. If he didn't know something, after making up his facts, he repeated them over and over so that in time it became the truth and because of his growing influence few people disputed him. Reg's reputation came in handy when there was work to be done or money to be made. He usually got someone else to do it for him for a tenth of the price while he claimed he originated the whole idea and pocketed the profits. He was always after a quick quid and he would lie, cheat and steal to get it.

Reg was also not above blackening someone's name to advance himself or to gain an advantage over them either. The more money he amassed the more he had to have and his methods became more ruthless and dishonest as time moved on. He was desperate for a new idea so he could profit from it because, after all he had his reputation to uphold and Rae and Amanda to keep sweet.

Reg and Rae were founding members of what the media, after they lost their fear of being sued into silence by the Preacher and his followers, dubbed the white shoe brigade. His last "new idea" would be his undoing and Reg would be held accountable for it one day but today was not the day.

Rae was the spitting image of her daughter but as she aged it cost Reg a fortune to maintain her fountain of youth. Rae was always more than happy to go along with Reg. She was no slouch either at turning a quotation to her advantage when anyone cast aspersions on Reg's business dealings. "All's fair in love and war," she used to say with a steely smile as she brandished her bible. It was the only printed word they were allowed to read as their Preacher had told them books had killed his brother. Reading had to be avoided unless it was necessary. Rae and her Christian group lobbied relentlessly on his behalf, insisting children didn't go to school to learn how to read or to think. They went to school to learn what to think.

I joined Dad behind the bar as he got some more lemon squash for Mum.

'Seems to me that more and more of them right–winger blow–ins from overseas are joinin' up with them squatters and gettin' into government. None of them believes they belong in this country among the workin' people. They're hell bent on gettin' rid of everythink we sweated for so the rich can get richer. They're back on their hobby horse that the unions are giving worker's money to communism and the Labor Party.'

Dad took the drinks over to his guests.

Rae went to church twice on Sunday but as one of the pub patrons unkindly remarked that it was only because she was mad about one of the members there. "It's a love that dare not speak its name," he'd added darkly. "Not that you could speak it around them bible–bashers anyhow. They'd string you up."

No-one knew how Rae managed to cuckold Reg at every turn without his becoming aware of it but it seemed to add some much–needed spice to her life. Reg seemed oblivious about most things except gouging money with the only original idea he had ever had—getting other people to give him theirs for nothing. It required his full attention.

Rae would not hear a word said against Reg. "He's the genius of the family," she told everyone and she was but his handmaiden, carrying out his orders. "I'm only fulfilling my marriage vows," she told people who asked her why, as one of the holiest women in town, she went along with what Reg was up to. "Love, honour and obey."

Dad was shaking his head.

'That excuse didn't hold up at Nuremberg, Rae,' he said.

It soon became clear she didn't know who or what Nuremberg was. She certainly knew it wasn't in Queensland. As long as Rae could bask in Reg's reflected glory, spend his money, claim her share of the credit, intimidate shop assistants with an icy, "Don't you know who I am?" and continue with her dalliances, she was quite content with pretending she was very happily married and on the right side of the gods. Rae was rather impressed with the Preacher too.

'He certainly knows a lot of people in high places, doesn't he?' She confided to Dad.

"Yair. Didn't one of them build Wolf's Lair right on the top of one of them Bavarian mountains?' He had a wicked grin on his face. 'That's where most of them politicians like the Preacher git their ideas from, don't they?'

Mum gave Dad a furious look, warning him to cut it out and to stop baiting people.

'Well, it's a good thing, getting guidance from the Mother Country.' Rae prattled on. 'I mean, we are quite isolated from the latest fashions.'

'At least he's stopped the communists from taking over.' Reg made his contribution to the conversation. 'I won't do business with anyone who's had anything to do with a union.'

Dad nodded his head.

'Yair. No unions. No protests. No free press. No opposition. No decent wages. No rights. No say in the joint. No point in voting. Don't you worry about that?'

Rae and Reg laughed as they recognised their Preacher's favourite saying. 'He really gives it to them, doesn't he?'

Dad was disgusted. His conversation and insights had bounced right off them.

'Serves you right,' Mum hissed as she picked up the glasses.

She turned to her guests.

'Would you like another drink? Some more nuts?'

Rae and Reg shuffled around.

'We'd better get a move on. We have to take Amanda to get the last fitting done on her dress.'

Amanda flounced down the steps with Henry following behind her.

'Oh look,' she turned to Henry with a smile. 'It's plain Jane the Super Brain.'

She was delighted with her turn of phrase.

'Written anything fascinating lately, Jennifer, or better yet, saleable?'

Baby Girl scowled around the corner. Jake had brought her down for the wedding. Amanda went over to her, then roughed her fingers through Baby Girl's hair. Furious Baby Girl combed it down again.

'How are you, Belinda?'

Amanda made her name an obscenity too. She enjoyed tormenting Baby Girl. She touched her on the arm. Baby Girl rubbed it off. Laughing, Amanda looked at my broom.

'Are you sweeping with it?' she asked. 'Or are you going for a ride on it?'

Henry pulled Amanda away then pushed her through the doorway to where her parents were waiting.

'She's not the boss.' Baby Girl was angry. 'Big bitch.'

I began to playfully sweep her up with some leaves.

'After tomorrow you don't have to worry about it. Henry will be married and Jake will take you back home.'

'I want to stay here.'

Baby Girl sounded mutinous.

No. No.

'You can't, BG.'

I tried to think of some excuses that didn't involve Mum's abuse or Dad's drinking.

'Besides, you'd have nowhere to put Rebel. You and Jake are getting on alright, aren't you?'

Baby Girl's shoulder slumped. I hesitated, unsure of how far I could go with the conversation.

She's forgotten what it's like.

'Maybe in a few years BG, after you've finished high school. Maybe Mum and Dad will have sorted things out by then. Maybe you can see them during school holidays.'

I searched desperately for a more convincing reason.

'Besides Amanda will be here all the time and you'd hate that, wouldn't you?'

She walked away. She'd also refused to be the flower girl or to wear a dress so we were relegated with Jake at the back of the church. In our brown and black, we looked like a row of Australthorp crossbreeds perched on a roost in the henhouse. On the right we're Reg and Rae's relatives. On the left were ours.

Beautiful bouquets of white flowers had been attached to the pews with white satin ribbons. Rose and jasmine perfumed the air. Reg and Rae had wanted the Preacher to marry Amanda but at the last minute, he'd had to cancel, fortuitously avoiding a punch–up from the relatives who disputed his policies.

Dressed in a morning suit, Henry stood at the top of the altar with Uncle Harry and Dad.

Henry has no friends.

The relatives were out in force but Henry should've had a friend to be the best man. Perhaps he'd been so busy saving Mum he'd never made one. Despite the church being crowded he cut a lonely figure.

The organist stopped fiddling around on the keys and struck up *The Wedding March*.

We stood then turned to see a tiny pink flower girl strewing red rose petals from a fancy cane basket in front of Amanda's feet. Baby Girl curled her lip; there but for fortune the pink flower girl would've been her.

Amanda had her arm tucked into her father's as she shimmered in white silk at the doorway. The bridesmaids paled into pink behind her. Amanda began to simper down the aisle nodding to this person and that but no matter how much effort Amanda had put into her wedding outfit, Mum'd put more into hers.

Her friend, Violetta had got it from Paris.

It was sheer nearly white Chantilly lace over pale Jordan almond satin, rounded in a daring décolletage. It was tied with a white satin ribbon just a smidgen above her waist. The dress flowed out from there, fluttering around her every movement as if carried by hundreds of tiny white butterflies.

In contrast to the large hats the other women had on their heads, Mum wore a white turban. When she stood she appeared to be taller than Dad. Her feet were shod in almond satin stilettos. She wore her mother's black opals on her ears and neck. The light caught their red, gold, and green fire. Her cigarettes were inside an almond satin handbag. Dad looked as proud as punch as he stood beside her. He touched her lightly and lovingly this way and that as he brought out the best in her for the congregation to envy.

Amanda gritted her teeth as she went past Mum to limpidly make her way to the altar. As Reg handed her over to Henry we sat down. A hush fell over the church. Baby Girl put her hand in mine for a few seconds. I squeezed it softly. Jake took her other one. Jake's husband put his arm around both of them. I knew they'd look after Baby Girl with every breath in their bodies. Even though the scene in front of me had disaster written all over it there was no stopping Henry or telling him to go back now.

I'll never get married. Ever.

Henry and Amanda came back to the hotel after their honeymoon. Soon afterwards Reg was arrested for corruption. He thought he'd been really smart by putting all his money into Rae's bank account. The Preacher and his mob wouldn't be able to get their hands on it and neither would the person who'd launched the lawsuit.

'It's pretty difficult to get arrested for rortin' in this State,' Dad remarked as he busied around the bar. 'God knows, it's open slather here. He must've really put someone's nose out of joint. Stole the words out of some poor bugger's mouth I bet.'

While Reg protested his innocence Rae took off with a lady from the church. They moved to India with Reg's money where they formed the Our God is Greater Missionary Association so they too could wave an aspirin around the dying, take it themselves and call it charity. But, as Aunty Gloria pointed out they'd be very wealthy people in a very poor country so they'd be able to live the life of Riley for quite a long time as Big Whiteys lording it over the dark people.

She also told me that Uncle Lincoln and his brother, Lionel had got jobs up on the property she and Uncle Rhodie were working on. It was where Moonlight and his mob used to set out from to walk down the river so they were more than happy to be back on country.

Reg couldn't mount much of a defence without money or dobbing in half the country so after being found guilty he was given fifteen years. With good behaviour the Judge told him, he could get out in ten. While Amanda begged her father to be good, Reg just continued to look disgusted for having been snookered in the first place by people he considered rank amateurs. For the life of him he couldn't muster any contrition for what he'd done. He thought he had every right to do what he did. All he was guilty of was diddling a mug. Reg and Rae were soon forgotten in the excitement of Amanda's sudden announcement that she was pregnant. Henry was over the moon. After the fuss died down Amanda was left with the reality of being pregnant, her changing size, and her impending responsibilities. She faked her way through the joy of it all.

Mum and Dad's new city life was supposed to be their retirement— their golden years. Mum was popular on the piano and Dad was still undefeated at the bar. Neither wanted to give it up or be grandparents but Henry ran himself ragged trying to please Amanda. It didn't take Dad long to realise that he was the breadwinner again—for all of them— Mum, Henry, Amanda, Baby Girl and a new baby.

When Amanda had a boy Henry was besotted with him but not as smitten as Dad. He adored Young Tom from the second he saw him. He did everything for him while Henry waited on Amanda. She'd taken to her bed exhausted from her efforts but on my visit there I could see that, even after a week, Amanda was beginning to tire of the baby. She was more than glad that Dad had taken him over.

After I went back to Sydney again I'd whittled my life down to writing. I set myself up again with a typewriter, dictionaries, ribbons, pens, pencils, and paper. I applied the same discipline I'd learned when I played the piano. I was determined to make a go of something. One morning shortly after I got back from visiting Mum and Dad, there was a knock on the front door. Everyone had gone to work. Scared stiff I looked through the peephole. Amanda was outside it with Young Tom.

'I was so frightened I didn't know where else to go.'

Amanda spoke in the little girl gush she'd adopted to get her own way.

'Henry bashed the baby. I am so terrified about what your father's going to do if he finds out.'

She shoved her way inside.

'I couldn't think of anywhere else to go.'

She was evaluating my surroundings.

'Henry hit the baby?'

I didn't mean to sound as disbelieving as I did.

Amanda picked up on the tone of my voice as she dropped her shoulder bag down on the carpet in the lounge room.

'You don't think I did it, do you?'

She looked hurt and lost.

She handed the baby over to me while she got out a cigarette. When I looked at Young Tom he had a fading red mark on his little face. He'd obviously copped a wallop. He stared at me with his big blue eyes. I stroked the top of his carrot red hair then twirled it into tiny curls.

I gave a short laugh.

'Well I don't think Henry did. Henry couldn't and wouldn't hurt a fly.'

Amanda dropped the little girl persona.

'Fuck you.'

She lit her cigarette.

'You've got no idea what it's like. I can't do anything at all except put up with that thing and Henry, not that they'll believe him anyway.'

You're not getting away with it.

'Amanda, you've got what you wanted. You've got the baby. You've got Henry. You've got people to pay for you and put a roof over your head. But, you must know by now that's there's no such thing as a free lunch.'

The phone rang. Amanda jumped dramatically.

'Don't tell anyone where I am.'

Dad was on the line.

'Is the baby alright?'

'Yes he is.'

I juggled Young Tom on my hip.

'Tell her to come back. I've got rid of Henry.'

'What do you mean you got rid of Henry? He didn't do anything. Amanda hit the baby. Henry didn't do it. What did you do to him?'

'He's not going to come anywhere near that baby ever again.'

Dad ignored what I'd said.

'Tell her to come home.'

He hung up.

Amanda smirked as I put the phone down.

'Told you your father'd believe me over Henry. Your father will do anything to hang onto the baby because he's got nothing else. He'll do anything I want. And this.'

She took Young Tom from me.

'You're going to look after Mummy, aren't you?'

I took her back to the airport.

She went to hug me before she boarded but I stepped away from her.

Not long after, without telling Mum, Dad sold the hotel and bought a grazing property back in the town.

Mum'd reacted by going from dentist to dentist trying to get one to agree to take out all her teeth. She'd told me she'd been looking in the mirror and decided years of cigarette smoking and tea drinking had irrevocably stained them. She'd thought if she got false teeth she could smoke and drink as much tea as she liked because she'd always have dazzlingly white teeth simply by soaking them in Steradent. I'd tried to talk her out of it by telling her that she needed her original teeth to stop her face from falling in but she wouldn't listen.

With her mother in India and her father in Boggo Road Jail Amanda didn't mind living in the bush. Dad'd brought her a car so she could go into town whenever she wanted to. She finally achieved the only ambition she'd ever had—to be a big fish in a little pond. Unfortunately it was also Mum's goal and she already occupied the pond.

Henry tried and tried to remain in contact with Young Tom. He'd drive out to the town on Friday night, getting there by Saturday morning. He'd go to the property to be greeted by Dad with a rifle in his hands and Amanda smirking triumphantly as she held the baby out of his reach.

Mum refused to have anything to do with him. After a quick visit to Baby Girl he'd sleep at Uncle Darcy's place on Saturday night then drive back to the city to start work on Monday so he could send money to support both Amanda and his son. Henry told me that he'd wait until Young Tom grew up. After that happened he hoped Young Tom'd like to get to know him.

Amanda was prepared to do anything to protect her lie, her status, and her lifestyle. She was determined to keep Young Tom as far away from Henry as she could, for as long as she could, and by any means. She had finally landed on someone else's feet and she was going to use anything and everything to stay on them. Young Tom would get to know Henry over her dead body.

Dad usually took Young Tom with him wherever he went. When he was on horseback Young Tom sat on the saddle in front of him. This was just as well as neither Mum nor Amanda could stand him. I went out to visit them to try to get them to let Henry see his son. They wouldn't discuss it.

Mum and Dad had turned away from each other and Amanda made sure they'd stay that way. All Dad had to cling onto now was Young Tom. At nearly sixty his body was wracked with cramping back pain from years of hard yakka and shearing. He spent his nights walking around trying to ease the pain. He refused to acknowledge how desperately hurt he was by Mum and Amanda's behaviour. Eye rolling expressed their complete and utter contempt for his best efforts at looking after them but Young Tom thought his grandfather was the greatest person he'd ever met.

On the days he couldn't mind Young Tom, Mum and Amanda were drafted into babysitting. They took turns at throwing whatever was handy at him to make him crawl as quickly as he could onto the back verandah where he'd wait for Dad to come home.

Amanda and Mum were forging a relationship where each mirrored the other—hatred of children bound them closer. On my short visits all I could do was make sure Baby Girl was not involved in it. Jake did her best to protect Baby Girl from the family without appearing to be keeping her away from them as I had asked her to.

Dad loved being back out in the bush. He was in his element there as a skilled bushman. Sheep and cattle prices were good. There was rain for once. I was relieved to find that although Aunty Gloria and Uncle Rhodie had decided to move to the city, Uncle Darcy, Uncle Lincoln, and Aunty Pearl were still in town as were other relatives. Dad wasn't completely friendless.

Uncle Darcy agisted his horses on Dad's property so he loaned me one to do help Dad out around the property.

While we were mustering Dad saw a young pig making a run for it through the mulga. With Young Tom positioned safely on the saddle Dad took off after it, weaving through the densely packed trees. When he caught up to it, he held Young Tom in one arm while he bent down to grab the pig by its hind leg with the other. The horse continued at a gallop. After he secured the pig Dad hauled himself back up into the saddle.

'Dinner,' he told Young Tom as he held him in one hand and the terrified pig with the other.

We reined our horses back into a canter.

Young Tom held on tightly to the mane and the pommel while Dad managed to manoeuvre the writhing pig and themselves back to the homestead. Mum still couldn't eat anything. Her gums wouldn't heal so her new teeth couldn't be fitted. Dad had been busy in the kitchen preserving and curing. He gave me a large portion of homemade bacon to take back to Sydney.

Shortly afterward the drought bit and the bottom dropped out of sheep and cattle prices. I posted Mum back tins of Sustagen so she could get some nutrition until she got false teeth. With four mouths to feed Dad went back to the brutal work of the shearing sheds to keep money coming in. No one would buy a drought-stricken property, and neither Mum nor Amanda would lift a finger to help him. Little bit by little bit as he grew older Young Tom began to take on the chores around the house. Amanda filled him up with fear and hatred of Henry. Without having even met his father Young Tom spat out loathsome phrases he'd picked up from Amanda. Mum laughed and Dad never stopped him.

Although everyone had wanted to believe her for their own purposes, Amanda's lie continued to contaminate everything it touched. As her lie grew alongside Young Tom it began to strangle the life out of everyone who came into contact with it.

Henry started to find solace in grog.

And like so many of our relatives he eventually disappeared into the bottle and, after a brief struggle with it, he stayed there.

SIMPLE SIMON

The Id rocked the night at a club near Taylor Square. Jeff St John's creamy honeysuckled voice soared through the crowd with the precision and phrasing of an ancient bluesman. He was heartbreakingly howling through Hummingbird when the air turned cold and shivery and then into Rupert.

I ducked under a table to hide and pulled what I thought was a tablecloth over my head. It turned out to be a pale blue oversized man's shirt. The owner of it spoke down the sleeve.

'Hello. Are you alright down there?'

My heart was thumping out of my chest. My skin felt covered in bruises and gravel rash. I'd broken out in plague-like pustules.

'Are you in trouble?'

He had an English accent.

'No.'

Slowly a part of me split off from the panic and began to think in a cold detached manner.

'So, you do this often?'

'I'm sorry. I thought you were a tablecloth.'

The Englishman had startling white skin. I decided to take a quick look to see if Rupert was around as well as check the nearest exits then make a run for it. How did he know I was here?

You're so stupid. You told him you liked jazz and blues. Stupid.

The Englishman hesitated before he introduced himself.

'My name's Simon.'

I took a deep breath. 'J.'

We shook hands before he lifted up his shirt a little and I got out from underneath it. Rupert was standing against the wall watching the band. As if he were flicked onto the stage like a set of two-up coins Jeff spun silver as strobe lighting lit the wheels of his chair that whirled him around the stage. He pounded through Big Time Operator.

Rupert started scanning the room.

I ducked under the table again.

Simon grabbed me.

'Tell you what, how about I take you outside to get some fresh air?' He put his arm around me, which shoved my head into his armpit. His shirtsleeves almost covered my body. He moved me quickly through the crowd to the exit. 'I don't think he saw you.'

I removed myself from his arm. As we walked away from the hotel, The Small Faces strobed the streets with *Itchycoo Park* lilting it with a mischief and laughter that was always out of my reach.

'I live just around the corner from here,' Simon said. 'At the Mansions. How about I act as your guard for the night?'

I hesitated.

'I'm 'armless, guv, 'onest.

Yair right.

He spoke in such a self-deprecating way I laughed.

We walked into a boarding house then up some stairs while I made a number of plans to cover every possible scenario.

'Do you want the bed?' Simon asked as we went inside his room.

'The chair will do.'

I tried to quell the panic that was coming back now that I was in relative safety. I moved the chair to the door. Simon threw a couple of cushions my direction, got into bed and turned off the light. Sirens began to wail up and down the street.

'What did he do to you?'

'Nothing.'

From a small crack in the window blind I could see a star. How much money do I have? Where could I go to? My next shift wasn't until the afternoon so I had plenty of time to pack before I hit the road.

'You know running isn't going to do you any good.'

In the dark Simon had been reading my mind.

'It cost me ten pounds to get here from England. I found out the other night I've been called up to fight in Vietnam.'

I stuck a cushion behind my head.

'What are you going to do?'

His gold earring glittered in the dark.

'Object.'

The pacifists I'd read about had ended up in jail, or New Zealand.

'Maybe they can deport you but you probably wouldn't be allowed back.'

'Like that'd break my heart.'

Philippe'd told me that all the artists and writers were going to England. The crushing weight of living under the Menzies government from one year to the next had stifled the life out of everyone. His conservative party called it the golden age of liberalism.

Most Australians never got to see any glitter or glam not unless you went to a drag show in Oxford Street. Women still had no equity of any kind in our own lives let alone the country. The economy was kept going by migrants who worked as factory and farm fodder for next door to nothing. The blackfellas were not thought of as Australian and were despised in a way that made no sense. Their money was taken off them and held in a trust by a government you wouldn't trust as far as you could throw it. Like Stalin's Russians we too had bodgie black and white television sets, clapped-out locally manufactured cars, no sewerage and a ferocious censorship placed on nearly every aspect of our lives.

Philippe took full advantage of the Menzies era. He loved the way most things were banned. He catered to his clienteles' every whim. Their whims were astonishing. Mesmerized by his French accent, food and sophistication, artists'd accepted Philippe's offer to mind their paintings and furniture for them while they went to the Mother Country. With his borrowing this and that and his volunteer work, Philippe'd eventually ended up with an exceptionally valuable and important art collection, plus a house full of antique furniture as well as his various businesses.

'If 'omosexuality wasn't against the law,' Philippe'd explained his light-fingered activities to us at the time, 'I'd never've been forced to become a crook,' he said.

He was very hurt by our outburst of laughter.

I tried to make polite conversation with Simon.

'What do you do in England?

'Nothing much. My parents are gypsies so we mainly travel around in caravans.'

You're no more a gypsy than I am.

The Roms used to come to town with the travelling shows to sell us their homemade wooden clothes pegs and wild horses. They were a tight knit group and all of them were linked by blood. They most certainly weren't related to Simon.

'What do you do?' Simon asked drowsily.

'I'm going to be a writer.'

'What genre do you specialise in?'

'What've you got?'

But Simon'd drifted off to sleep.

Shards of sunlight hit my face. I smoothed myself down and tried to exit Simon's room as quietly as I could.

'Do you have a phone number?'

Simon'd opened one eye.

I briefly thought about writing it down back to front but I tore a piece of paper from my notebook and scribbled it down.

'I share a place.'

Simon tucked it under his pillow and went back to sleep.

After I freshened up in the communal toilet at the end of the hallway I waited inside the boarding house until a bus came along. At the last minute I jumped on it, changed in the city and constantly checking over my shoulder I travelled back to the house. As far as I could see Rupert hadn't followed me.

In my bedroom I quietly rolled my things into a swag, checked my bankbook was still in my purse and put a few notebooks of writing in it. I took it to the shower with me just in case. Too afraid to put my face under water for more than a second in case I missed seeing him I nervously checked every shadow.

Kitty was waiting when I came out of the bathroom.

'Are you going somewhere?'

She followed me into my bedroom and sat on my mattress.

'Were you going to tell us?'

I gave her the only answer I could.

'No.' I hesitated. 'I have to go.'

'I thought we were all getting on pretty well.' Kitty was hurt. 'Why?'

I sat on my empty suitcase.

'No reason.'

'Is it to do with that guy who turned up here yesterday?'

The bottom fell out of my world. It seemed my life'd always be dark and flat and spent running—running and cleaning.

'It is, isn't it? We pissed him off and told him not to come back. He didn't like it very much. He said to tell you he's got a job at the hospital.'

I can't go back there.

I tried to get out one word at a time.

'I don't want to cause you any trouble. He won't go away. So I will.'

'Philippe'll deal with him. He used to be in the French Foreign Legion.'

'He was a cook.'

'Cook, crook, whatever. You have to be a bad bugger to be in Algiers in the first place. So stay. Philippe'll enjoy taking him on anyway. He's bigger than him.'

The phone's shrill ring from the lounge room caused me to jump. Nancy answered it. I tried to explain Rupert to Kitty.

'He's tried to kill me on a number of occasions. I don't want to cause any of you harm. I don't know who he is really or what else he is capable of.'

'I suppose you went to the police.' She read my face. 'Useless bastards.' She got up off the bed. 'Then it's Philippe.'

Or Perth or Madrid.

Nancy came into the room.

'Some guy called Simon is on his way over.'

'So is Philippe.' Kitty said. 'Reinforcements.'

She put her arm around me.

'Let's make some coffee and laugh until they get here.'

She led me out into the kitchen and handed me a ginger nut biscuit.

'We'll take you in shifts. Make sure you're not alone.'

I had doubts about their plan but mine was no better. I stayed. So did Simon.

At first it was sugar and spice and all things nice that's what little girls are made of; then snakes and snails and puppy dog's tails that's what little boys are made of.

It turned into semen dance of snake upon snake entwined for hour upon hour; heads shadowing on skin, dappling softly on the sheets; muscle sweetly sweating on muscle; sighing shivering slithering scale skin and semen syrup turning into sleep; waking fitfully through the night to look longingly at him.

When he spoke and smiled it fitted in to me with a familiarity I thought was love, and because it was love, I skipped over his glib behaviour and the glaringly obvious.

The only thing he had told the truth about was the fact he'd been conscripted into the Army. For the best part of a year his ill-thought out but wide-ranging lies covered everything from being a heroin addict, a gypsy, a street person and an artist-musician. Any thought I had about meaning something to him was lost in them but he kept Rupert away. Nothing Simon said could be relied on but then I didn't expect any better from him or anyone else.

Everything I'd ever wanted had been taken away by Rupert. I couldn't get it back again. I had to accept second best or worse, third rate. No matter what I did it would never redeem me or allow me to get any further than I was now.

Mum'd told me not long ago that I belonged in the gutter with all the other gutter people and Amanda had laughed. Dad'd drummed his fingers on the table, and Young Tom'd made himself scarce. The only person life was going well for was Baby Girl. She'd passed her exams and had begun to work as a nurse at the hospital. She still lived with Jake and the animals they rescued.

Although Rupert made his presence known around the hospital, once he knew about Simon, he pretended he'd changed from menacing to mate. We were old friends. He'd introduced me to one of the nurses he had begun to date. She was blonde, tall and angular but try as I might I couldn't avoid them all the time.

'Rupert told me he met you in Mount Isa.'

She fingered a large gold cross around her neck and spoke as if I were a discarded girlfriend. I decided for the first time since it happened to say something.

'He raped me in Mount Isa and then tried to kill me on three occasions. He has followed me for years. He won't go away. You should be very careful of him.'

She laughed at me.

'If I believed my finance was capable of that I wouldn't be with him. If he had done that to you why are you still hanging around him, chasing after him, trying to get him back?'

She handed me a wedding invitation.

'Rupert wants you there though god knows why after that outburst. He warned me you were the jealous type.'

When I got home from work Simon was in his favourite pose, playing the dulcimer as the son of gypsies. He sang softly to himself. I was going to tell him I thought I was pregnant but a letter written in ornate handwriting on my bed side-tracked me. Puzzled I picked it up as I sat down.

'It's from my girlfriend.'

Simon strummed the strings with a plastic pick.

'We're getting married as soon as I get back to England in a few weeks or so.'

I glanced at the letter.

'She's ten years older than me and she has three children.'

He kept on playing for a while.

'She's really talented and very gifted as you can see. It's not easy to write in that ornate style of handwriting.'

He struck a few more notes.

'I suppose I should've told you sooner.'

When I didn't reply he continued.

'It must be difficult for you to think that I'd be attracted to someone older than either of us.'

No. That isn't the difficulty. It's the year and a bit you've been living off me.

As he talked I slowly slipped back into the dust and darkness where I had no meaning. In the nothingness I decided I had a choice—to live or die or to kill myself working to provide everything I could for something and somebody that was mine—that couldn't be taken away from me.

Simon continued to come around until it was time for him to go back to England. As we went down to the ship to say goodbye he told me that if ever I was in England to look him up. No hard feelings. I told him casually I thought I was pregnant. He shrugged as if he couldn't care less. He waved farewell from the deck and threw a streamer.

Philippe'd told me all men were lying bastards and he should know. His lies dripped off his tongue like honey. I told him that I'd failed cookery and sewing at school, and as I had six months or so to wait until the baby arrived, I'd go see the world instead of knitting booties.

Don and Trisha were already in London so I'd have somewhere to stay when I got there. Ben, our Canadian friend who was on his way back home had also offered his support. Kitty, Nancy, Ben, John and Philippe threw a giant farewell party and on the weekend Rupert got married, I sailed forth on the seven seas to Europe, free at last. I had enough money in my kick to last a year or so. I rarely spent any money on myself. I was going to do whatever I liked whenever I liked or for at least for the next few months.

Seasickness nearly killed me.

I couldn't get off the bunk nor could I smoke anymore. A French waiter came down to the cabin three times a day with some form of sustenance he thought I could hold down. I fainted in Fiji and didn't get off the bunk until we got to the Americas.

The French waiter helped me up on the deck so I could watch the ship sail through the concrete blocks of the Panama Canal. They completely dwarfed us. Panama reminded me of the town and how insignificant I'd always felt in The Outback under its blanket of stars and smoke.

Rows of little wooden houses came into view.

Everyone was dressed in their Sunday best as they sat outside on their verandahs in the growing dark. It looked like The Mish and suddenly I wanted to go home except I knew you couldn't go home once you'd left. I decided to get off the boat in Jamaica. I didn't know much about it except they'd thrown the British out in a declaration of independence, had terrific music, some of it sung by the Pindar Family.

The captain broadcast a warning over his PA system.

'We advise everyone for their own safety only to go to the Hilton Hotel.'

He repeated it three times.

A steel band played on the docks. I heard a young British lad ask if anyone wanted to go to the Hilton.

'Nah.' His friends wanted adventure. 'Let's walk around to see the real Jamaica. We might run into Sir Frank Worrell.'

'Or Garry Sobers.' The young British lad was hopeful.

I was desperate to walk so when they asked I went with them. We picked up some more travellers on the way. With each step I felt stronger. Before we got very far people started shouting at us then began to push us into the gutter. The footpaths belonged only to the Jamaicans they shouted. The British began to march along the gutters. We followed them somewhat bemused.

The people were desperately poor and their shops bereft of goods. It seemed Britain had sucked the country dry on its way out.

As I walked along it struck me that most of Dad's brothers and sisters were black. I'd always known they were black but I hadn't really thought about them being black before. What was it like to be black when the majority now was white? How did two Scots have so many black children? Who were they? Where did they come from? At most I'd probably spoken to my parents, my family and the people of the town for a total of about six months during my whole life. I didn't know who anyone was. There were over twenty-six black, white and brindle people in Dad's family. A few more from Mum's.

One of the guy suggested we duck into a café to get out of the heat, the dust and away from the angry people. The café looked respectable enough. We walked in and sat down at a table.

A band was playing. People appeared to be having a good time, dancing and singing along. Some bottles of drink arrived on our table. We paid in American dollars. We didn't get any change from them. The drink appeared to be a local cola. As I tapped my fingers in time to the music I glanced in the mirrors that hung behind the band. They reflected behind us were wall-to-wall broken bottles being held by people who didn't want us there. The band began to falter.

I turned to my fellow travellers.

'Do any of you know how to fight?'

I casually drained my bottle of cola and slipped it up my sleeve as everyone saw what I had in the mirrors.

The only thing we could rely on was the element of surprise.

'On the count of three. One, two …'

And then we were right near the broken bottles, through them and out of the street. We began to run. We tried and tried to hail the taxis that cruised by us. They wouldn't stop. We could hear the mob howling behind us. We rounded a corner and finally a taxi slowed.

'Where you from?' the driver asked.

'Switzerland.'

'I was told there were some British here trying to cause trouble.'

We climbed in the cab. 'We yodel and ski.'

He drove us back to the boat.

The steel band demanded money from us and we finally made it up the gangway. Weeks later we passed the white cliffs of Dover and I'd arrived in the Land of the Pointy Nosed People as Lincoln called them. They looked the same as me but they were not. Their houses looked the same but they were not. This was not my country and I did not belong here. I wanted to go back to my country.

England was even poorer and dirtier than Jamaica with most people waiting in long, defeated lines for everything they wanted to ask for or buy. It seemed that only the upper echelons of Britain had made money from all the wars, sacrifices and conquests. The ordinary people hadn't made a penny.

However, just in case their fortunes rose again, they'd developed a desperate need to hang onto who they once thought they were, despite their current circumstances. When they heard our accents they immediately became snobbily better than we were, more educated, more sophisticated and more knowledgeable although they had rarely left the suburbs they were born in.

They could only afford to shower once a week, that is if they had running water. Their bathtubs were filled with coal to ward off the bitter winter cold and they used a sponge at the kitchen sink to keep clean.

Trisha and Don'd greeted me effusively and made up a bed on the floor. I threw my swag down and we began to yarn about being here and being back in our own place. Home. Every day I was covered in a fine sooty dust that was difficult to get off. Overcome with desperation to eat Asian food, some people recommended the Chinese Quarter in Soho. It has the best Chinese food in London or England, if the truth be told, they said. The waiter asked me if I wanted chips with my black bean stir-fry.

For a people who had conquered most of the world it seemed they hadn't incorporated any of its knowledge into their lives. Pumpkin was only fed to cattle and the food they did eat was stewed and boiled until there wasn't an ounce of nutrition left in it. Although Carnaby Street was supposed to be leading the world in food, fashion, and music, it wasn't all that different from Australia's King's Cross or Oxford Street.

I finally decided that everyone thought it had to be great because it was called Great Britain and no one could bear to think of it any other way. Like the lucky country and the American dream the British would rule the waves again just not today. They were only temporarily on their uppers.

Don and Trish were on the tail end of their trip around the world, and Don told me he was going to settle down with Trisha. She had confided that as both were Catholics they had decided to have at least six children. I told her I'd decided only on the one. I couldn't afford any more.

After I got in touch with Simon, his mother invited me to see her. Trisha and Don farewelled me and wished me luck. We'd met up again in Sydney.

Simon's mother had a large middle-class house surrounded by a large middle-class well-kept garden. She didn't think much of Simon but she told me he had married and neither she nor he wanted me to interfere with their lives. Pissed off, I wrote to him several times not realising he would keep my letters to show his child one day. He wrote back to say he was busy protesting against nuclear war and didn't want to see me but he asked the child be named Rene, the same name as my mother, if I had a girl. I'd decided to call her after Baby Girl or rather Baby Girl's middle name, Gemma. I never thought about having a boy.

I lived on the streets and fields of England and Eire throughout the summer until Gemma was born. I wasn't going to waste money on rent when I knew how to survive without having to. The hairs rose on my neck when I visited the hospitals for a checkup. I avoided those with a cross out front. I suspected they'd behave just as they had when I worked in them. They'd take my life off me and hand me one they had made up and then try to beat me into acceptance of it. Hell would freeze over before I went anywhere near them.

Just as the Aboriginal women had told me my body became pins and needles. I went to the local hospital, aware only of breathing down to the baby before pushing Gemma out. While Donovan sang *The Hurdy Gurdy Man,* the giant Ferris wheel outside my window provided me with multi-coloured lights and music. While the rest of the women were being encouraged to grunt, groan, scream or sign papers they knew nothing about, I had Gemma effortlessly in twenty minutes.

Simon had no interest in claiming paternity or allowing me to claim any on his behalf. He also told me he wouldn't pay anything towards her upkeep either. I took this as a sign that Gemma belong solely to me until she could belong to herself. His disinterest was a relief. I knew I could provide everything she wanted.

Before the mealy-mouthed could get their hands on me I removed Gemma from her crib when the nursing shift changed over for the afternoon and I was gone.

I sent a letter to Mum and Dad telling them that they were grandparents. On postcards I told Lincoln and Baby Girl that I had Gemma and everything was working out fine.

Out on the road again where no one could find me or take my life away we travelled to Eire where I knew some people. I worked as a private night nurse for the only British service member who had a map on how to get out of Burma when the Japanese invaded it. Everyone else was captured and put to work on the Thai-Burma railway. The Colonel had well-planned dementia as well as well-thought out incontinence and a cook. I spent the nights washing and changing him, feeding Gemma and waiting until she could travel.

I wrote copious letters with photos enclosed to everyone I knew in Sydney. After I had replenished my money I went to Canada to meet up with the lovely friend I had known in Sydney, Ben. When I got to Canada we instantly began talking where we'd left off in Sydney and soon we were sleeping together. Ben told me that in order to stay in Canada I'd have to marry him. I'd thought perhaps I'd judged marriage a bit too harshly and finally we did so on the proviso the whole thing was a bit of a joke in order for me to get a visa.

I wore a slight lemon Mary Quant shift dress and carried Gemma on my hip to the wedding. His friends were all stoned. Afterwards we went to his parents' house. I opened a cupboard in the kitchen to get some glasses. Dozens and dozens of bottles of spirits filled every square inch of space. My blood ran cold. When we got back to the motel we were staying in Ben began married life. He sat down in a chair then turned on the TV.

'Fetch me a cup of coffee, will ya?'

I looked at the life he was expecting to me to live.

'Fetch it yourself.'

And the marriage was over. It took several more months for it to fall to pieces. I arrived back in Sydney with Gemma to a welcome home party from Philippe and John in just under two years after I left.

Northwesterly winds, the scents of summer and the milky-white stars reminded me of home and I telephoned.

Dad answered the phone. He asked me when I could come up to visit. He couldn't wait to meet Gemma.

I told him I couldn't wait to get there.

THE WILD HORSE

'You needn't think I'm going to be a grandmother to that thing.'

Mum made me want to turn around and go home but Dad already had Gemma in his arms stroking her lightly on her cheek.

Did he do that with us?

'It's illegitimate.'

It'd taken me twenty-hours to get there. I'd arrived in my usual state—overwhelmed with excitement, sick from anxiety, filled with gut-wrenching fear, boofheaded and wrong. I tried to keep a lid on it.

Mum was dressed in immaculate fawn pants, a beige silk shirt and brown stilettoes.

Gemma had been sick down the front of my shirt.

'Having a child out of wedlock. An unwed mother. You're a disgrace.'

Mum stuck her nun-like finger out at Gemma.

'She can call me Aunt Rene.'

She pointed to Dad.

'And you, you can be Uncle Thomas. And you.'

Her face wrinkled in disgust.

'You can consider yourself lucky you're even allowed show your face back here.'

Dad drummed his fingers on the table. Wide–eyed, Gemma watched Mum's every move. Amanda smirked as she smoked her cigarette and drank what smelled like Scotch from her teacup.

'You're just like Robert Mitchum.'

Mum continued to seethe.

'You think?'

I turned my being back home into a Dad-like tongue-in-cheek banter.

'He's a wonderful poet, songwriter, actor—you name it, he can do it. I'm so flattered,' I finished lightly.

'You needn't play the innocent. You know what I'm talking about.'

Her fury was escalating.

'He smoked that marijuana stuff as well. I read all about it in The Woman's Weekly. It's what you all do down in the city, isn't it? He ended up in jail for it and you've ended up with that thing.'

She furiously threw cushions and newspapers around the room as she tidied it.

Dad spoke up.

'He was pretty good in *The Night the Hunter,* Robert Mitchum.'

He had a twinkle in his eye as he explained the film to Amanda.

'He played a callous killer who posed as a preacher so he could get his hands on the money his friend had hidden. He was a real coot of a bloke.'

Mum glared at him.

'I suppose you think that's funny. You've got no consideration for Amanda or how she feels about her father still being in jail.'

Amanda forgave Dad with a sad smile that fired a warning shot across his bow.

'I don't want to cause any trouble,' she murmured.

Whiter than a ghost Baby Girl stared out the lounge room window. Her straw blonde hair stuck up on end as if she had started to comb it then forgotten. Young Tom was out in the backyard trying to crack a whip. Baby Girl hadn't even acknowledged I was there. I looked around the room. None of the photographs of Gemma I'd sent was on display anywhere in the house. Only those of Young Tom took pride of place.

'I'll tell her the rules when she learns how to speak, Mum.'

I was still holding Gemma wondering if I should just go while the going was good.

'I only came up because Dad asked me too.'

Dad took Gemma again. He held her up in front of him.

'Grandpa. Grandpa.'

'Boomp. Boomp.'

Dad tried again.

'Grandpa.'

Gemma giggled and poked him in the cheeks with tiny fingers.

'Boompa.'

'Let's go down to the shops.'

Dad waltzed down the steps with her to the laundry where he kept the freezer. A few seconds later he came out with a tub of Neapolitan ice cream. Young Tom went over to join them. Dad bustled inside to get some spoons. In the shade of the passionfruit vine that grew over a trellis, Dad, Gemma and Young Tom dug into the tub of chocolate, vanilla and strawberry before it melted.

Mum went to the kitchen to make a pot of tea. I was going over to speak to Baby Girl when Amanda accosted me.

'I suppose you think by bringing that stinkin' little bastard up here you're going to cut me out of the family with it.'

She blew cigarette smoke in my face.

'It won't work. Her cute stage won't last. And you needn't think they're going to give you anything in their will either. Everything they've got belongs to me.'

I found my voice quickly. 'I pay my own way. I've never ever asked anyone for a cent. I don't bludge off anyone let alone an old man with a crippled back who needs to be in a rocking chair not out shearing to keep you. Why don't you go and mooch off your own parents? Why don't you go over to your mother in India or ask them for the money.'

I moved past her to Baby Girl.

'BG?'

I touched her on the shoulder.

'BG? Are you ok?'

Baby Girl stared at me for quite some time as if she didn't know who I was.

'BG, what's the matter? Why are you back here? I told you to stay away.'

'They're my parents.'

She sounded as if she hadn't spoken to anyone in years.

'You can't stay here, BG. Nothing has changed. Nothing. Not for you. Not for me. Come with me. I'll take you back to Jake's.'

Baby Girl was starting to focus on where she was.

'I can drive myself.'

She went back to staring out the window.

Amanda came over.

'She's always like that.'

She ruffled Baby Girl's hair roughly. Baby Girl didn't react.

'Nothing worse than being somewhere where you're not wanted, hey Belinda?'

Amanda lowered her voice.

'My son replaced all of you years ago. You'll never get back in. I'll make sure of it. You're not cutting me out of the will. They want us not you.'

'Tea's ready,' Mum called out from the kitchen.

'Coming Rene,' Amanda cooed in response.

I looked out the window with Baby Girl.

'I'm so sorry, BG.'

We watched Dad play with his grandchildren.

'She's right, you know. We have to make our own way. They can't help it. I don't know why they're like it. They just are.'

Young Tom stayed at the outdoor table with the melting tub of ice cream while Dad put a rainbow-coloured Gemma around his neck. He began galloping around—Dad the wild horse, my daughter the rider. His back bent him over. It took him a while to get his trot going. The old red dog that fell in by his side wasn't faring much better. Both of them were going bald, both had arthritis, fading eyesight and indifferent hearing. Red dog couldn't see or hear Dad's instructions anymore. Dad had told me red dog usually did all the farm work from memory. He always had a big gappy grin on his face while Dad yelled instructions and pointed. Dad's body had broken-down from years of hard work. Sadness prompted my arm around Baby Girl's thin shoulders. She remained rigid. Through Henry and me it seemed Dad was trying to be the sort of father he'd always wanted to be but wasn't with us.

Mum came out the back door in furious disapproval.

'I called you for tea.'

Dad galloped up to the steps and put a delighted Gemma down.

'Boompa.'

Mum looked at me.

'Just make sure that thing calls me Aunt Rene.'

She strutted on her high heels back into the kitchen, puffing on her cigarette.

I took Baby Girl and Gemma with me into the kitchen to have tea with the family. I tried to strike up a conversation with Mum while Dad dangled Gemma off the end of his foot to give her another horse ride.

'You're looking well, Mum.'

'Thanks to Amanda,' she snapped. 'If she hadn't brought me all those tins of Sustagen every week when she went into town I would've starved to death. She got the chemist to order them in. It was the only thing I could keep down.'

Amanda dared me to correct her. 'It was no trouble, Rene.'

While Baby Girl bit her fingernails I decided I wasn't going to bite my tongue.

'Did you get all the tins of Sustagen I posted from Sydney? I sent you dozens of them.'

Mum snorted in derision as if she didn't believe a word I was saying.

'I never got anything from you. We all know what you were too busy doing.'

She glared at Gemma.

'Well at least I've got my teeth in now.'

Amanda turned to me. 'And don't you think they look terrific Jennifer? So white and shiny.'

There was no point staying.

'I have to go back to Sydney. I've only got a few days off from work.'

'I suppose you don't get much time to write these days.'

Amanda set the trap for Mum.

'A couple of my stories have been made into plays.'

'People will put on any old rubbish these days, won't they?'

Mum tossed her head.

'They must be desperate.'

It was all they were going to get out of me.

'BG? How about we take Gemma into town so she can meet Jake?'

I took Gemma off Dad's foot and sat her on my lap. Dad looked stricken. I knew he wanted us to stay longer. Young Tom tried to sneak into the kitchen to join us. Amanda spotted him.

'You know better.'

Young Tom bolted outside again.

'You can come down to Sydney, Dad. Go to the races down there.'

Dad drank his tea.

Gemma stood up on me and began to give me butterfly kisses on my cheek. Mum shuddered.

'Make her stop that nonsense. It makes me sick to my stomach to see you two doing that. Pawing each other. Stop it.'

I put Gemma over my shoulder as I stood.

'Come on BG. Let's go.'

I turned to Dad.

'Do you need anything? I can bring it back out if you like.'

He shook his head. He looked as if he wanted to cry.

Mum and Amanda lit cigarettes. They puffed on them almost simultaneously, each movement synchronised. I didn't want Gemma around it. I didn't want any of us around it. I shook Dad's hand to say goodbye. He gave Gemma a kiss on her cheek then walked out to the verandah with us. Young Tom was sitting on the back step talking to himself. Dad stood alongside him.

'You go first BG. I'll follow you.'

After I strapped Gemma into her seat we waved goodbye as we drove out. I tailed Baby Girl down the corrugated road out of the property then turned onto the main stretch of gravel to go into town.

Like the river and The Glear that sometimes rose up from its ancient channel when the rains tumbled down everyone had to cut their own course. If I stayed around the family I'd be swirled into its muddy waters, dragged under and drowned. I had to strike out on my own and make a good life for both Gemma and me. After checking with Jake that Baby Girl would be looked after I drove away.

Years later I realised Baby Girl'd never forgiven me for that decision and the kundri of resentment and fear that festered inside her had begun to slowly and silently eat her life away.

STEVE

'Your luck's got to change one day.'

Philippe's booming sing–song voice introduced me to Steve. He shook my hand as Philippe continued.

'He's just been fired from the gig he had.'

'And how is that meant to be lucky?' I asked Philippe and John before I turned back to Steve. 'Why?'

Steve smiled endearingly. His long blonde hair flopped over one brown eye and the effect made him look quite frail. My heart went out to him. I tried to haul it back in.

Philippe explained.

'He can't dance.'

Steve chuckled. It was so carefree and infectious the rest of us laughed with him too. I wondered why Philippe was doing all the talking for him.

'Steve has a stammer. He's going to be like Piaf one day. You'll see. His voice is so magnificent. It makes me cry. He never stammers when he sing. People will die to hear him one day.'

John pursed his lips. 'Or something.'

Introducing me to Steve was clearly Philippe's idea.

We were sitting under the trellis in the backyard of Philippe's three–story Paddington house. Philippe's branching out from the tiny café he shared with his mother, Odette, into cash only gay male steam baths had more than made his fortune. John was still using the café as a meeting place for his frightened gay rights group. Philippe didn't agree with their politics because if homosexuality were legalised he'd find it difficult to make a living. Odette doted and devoted herself to both of them as well as her six Pomeranians. They were yapping around the backyard as Odette put baskets of bread on the red checked tablecloth. Wisteria hung down in giant purple bunches as bees buzzed lazily around them.

Philippe'd served his signature coq au vin. Trisha and Don along with Kitty and Nancy were sipping on rare reds while Philippe gave me tonic water with lime.

'So.' I laughingly challenged Steve, 'sing.'

Steve began to tap his foot to set a rhythm before he broke into a Jamaican fruit seller's song. It called everyone to come and sample the wares he had for sale in an enormous voice that belied his frail body. His sound changed the molecules in the air, hooked into every cell in my body and then turned it and my life upside down. I thought I'd fallen in love.

When he finished everyone at the table clapped.

'Listening to you Steve, is like drinking champagne. My 'eart is full of bubbles.'

Philippe was awestruck but John remained peeved. He exchanged "can you believe it" glances with Odette and pursed his lips some more.

Gemma came into the garden still half-sleepy from her nap. She climbed on Steve's lap and threw her arms around him then snuggled into his neck. She made it quite clear she did not want to be disturbed and Steve seemed quite content to let her stay there. Trisha and Don thought she was adorable, with her reddish blonde hair, giant green eyes, and upfront manner. They were having trouble conceiving. After she had her fill of Steve Gemma introduced herself to the other guests before settling on Odette.

Steve seemed genuinely interested in finding out about me. He was easy to talk too, mainly because he didn't say anything. He kept gesturing for me to keep talking. And without knowing how it happened I soon found myself alone with him, cut off from the rest of the guests. I was always unsure about who I was or if I had any right to be anybody but my babbling seemed to impress him. At twenty-four, by dint of my wits and hard work, I earned a living, reared a child, made some headway as a writer and occasionally composed songs. I also remained loyal to my friends and helped people who were down on their luck. Steve was down on his luck but as I was to learn a lot later, he was always down on his luck.

By the end of the afternoon I felt as if I'd known him forever and in a funny way, I felt a sense of responsibility for him and a slight worry about how he'd get on in life. When I thought about it years later I actually learned next-door to nothing about him that day except he sang and he was unemployed. He also smoked dope but in those days that was normal. Everybody had a joint now and then. I could take it or leave it. I didn't like it much. It wasn't as if it was alcohol.

Steve also indicated that, like me, he'd had a difficult relationship with his mother. I found out it too late that it extended to every mother, whether he knew them or not, but it wasn't on show that afternoon. After I'd fed Gemma she demanded Steve put her to bed. Steve joined me in singing the Pindar Family song, *And I Bid You Goodnight* to Gemma over the top of me while she fought against closing her eyes. Finally Gemma went to sleep and I tucked her in. I bent over to kiss the top of her curly strawberry blonde hair.

Steve burst into tears as if his hurt and sorrow was so deep nothing on earth'd ever fill it or heal it. Too late I learned later he was just a bottomless pit but that night I turned to see what I could do as he clung onto me. My mind filled in what he was unable to say and I wanted to give him all the love and affection he so obviously needed. As his tears dried, he began to kiss me as he undid the front buttons on my shirt.

I batted him away lightly. 'What about the courtship?'

'I think,' Steve hesitated to get his breath. 'I've fallen in love with you.'

With those magic words heard for the first time and as violins played softly underneath, the Dostoevsky–ish Russian romance between two people who barely knew each other, who couldn't distinguish instant intimacy from instant intensity, sex from love, or reality from fantasy, began. I'd synchronized with the unspoken in him and my life was about to be shipwrecked as I followed the sound of his siren songs.

Although Steve was a complete stranger I'd never felt safer or more loved by someone in all my life. He was a combination of all the books I'd ever read or movies I'd ever seen, the people I'd met—all played to beautiful music. I struggled to remember when I'd had that sense of safety before.

A memory of being out at a drover's camp with Dad when I was only three or four came to mind. The men had gathered around a bright campfire. Some were sitting on saddles, others their haunches. I leaned back into a burnished brown leather saddle and crossed my little legs to prevent them slipping into the fire. With fireflies fluttering above the flames and the men murmuring soothingly around me, I fell into a sleep so safe and so deep I never wanted to wake from it. I think it was the only night I hadn't sleep with one eye open or a foot on the floor.

I thought it had to be love at first sight with Steve even though it had a vaguely familiar edge that eluded an explanation.

While Steve hung out with Philippe, John, Gemma and me, we all completed his sentences for him. We said out loud what we thought Steve was thinking or what he had to say. Years passed before we realised that the Steve we had created had nothing to do with the actual Steve and everything to do with us. Soon he consumed all my time and nearly every ounce of space in my head.

After I moved into a small apartment to be nearer work and a day care for Gemma Steve told me how much he loved me and that he wanted to live with me. He looked like a small dog lost in the rain. I soon found myself managing his life for him because he appeared incapable of managing it himself. He was there every mealtime, helping himself to seconds. He was always sick with one ailment or another so it was never the right time to ask him to go. He always needed a lift here and there but never offered to pay for petrol.

It was difficult to write or play my small piano because as soon as I started Steve took it over to finish composing my music.

The lovemaking went all night long. I worked all day while he slept. As the scales tipped towards his career and coping with the people around him who idealised and idolised him, my life began to lose focus and meaning in exhaustion. I was falling out of love with him and his life. Finally, despite the fact he had the flu, I asked him to leave. It took him several days to organise somewhere to stay, with another woman, but eventually he was gone. A month or so later I began to suspect I might be pregnant.

'How it happened I don't know,' I confided in Philippe.

He raised an eyebrow.

'I mean, I'm on The Pill. I've never missed a day. I always take it at the same time. I don't want another child. I can't afford one.'

John piled some more salad on my plate.

'Steve probably swapped the pills with lollies or something. I never trusted that guy.'

Philippe protested.

'He's not that clever. His voice is magnificent but the rest of him is—' He frowned.

'Precisely.' John cut in. 'You don't know what the rest of him is.'

John pressed his point.

'Men cripple women's lives by getting them pregnant then they use the child to get access to the mother whenever they want. The woman has no choice but to put up with him. My mother did. She had eight kids. I bet you don't write much anymore either. All the women I know who had promising careers had to abandon them after they had children.'

'Or they became lesbians,' Philippe added helpfully.

'They were already lesbians,' John snapped but Philippe was deep in thought.

Not long after this conversation he opened ladies' only steam baths.

I had no intentions of doing an Amanda. I did not want another child and abortion offered me the choice to keep control over my life, my body, my career and my finances. I was determined not to tell Steve. It was none of his business and I wanted him out of my life.

Most men were conflicted about pregnancy. They knew if they controlled the womb they controlled the woman directly or indirectly for the rest of her life. While they benefitted from women's use of oral contraception, men objected to women having access to abortion when it didn't work. On the other hand when the father of the would-be bride suggested the shotgun wedding solution men objected to being tricked and trapped into providing a lifetime of lodging for a woman and her child. It was an appalling imposition on their inalienable right of freedom and it could ruin their lives.

God came to their rescue again.

The nuns'd take the babies from single women and adopt them out. Women'd forget about the child they had, childless couples would be overjoyed at having a baby and men could get on with their lives. Everyone could live happily ever after.

As I searched for a doctor, overnight the government stated no abortion'd be performed until they clarified the law that had been working quite well for some time. It stated a woman could abort a foetus if she said being pregnant was injurious to her brain or she was plain crazy. Doctors were threatened with the loss of their licences or jail if they assisted anyone. The parliamentarians were in no hurry to make a decision. My choices now were to adopt it or keep it.

Steve was back on my doorstep within minutes of the phone call from Trisha and Don with kisses, love and promises of changed behaviour. He never articulated what he was going to change into but he plugged into every insecurity I had through the information I'd originally given him. Gemma adored him and loved having him around. It also floated through my mind that I thought far more highly of Steve than he had ever thought of me.

With his stammer disappearing his ill-health and fragility was getting into full swing instead. Steve slowly began to reveal who he was in private to me while maintaining a public persona that was completely at odds with it. It had begun with how much he loved me but within days money began to disappear from my purse. Stoned from daylight to dark Steve's lies were endless. I feared people who were out of control on drugs or drink so I didn't understand why I had one living with me. It rendered me incapable of doing anything about him except hide what was going on and agree with the front that was presented to me. Gemma used to call it a 'false face' and it worried me that she could do very good imitations of it. Philippe was apologetic. He'd had no idea that Steve was such a rotter, a bounder.

'They say I'm a bastard, but he's a bigger bastard than me,' Philippe opined. 'At least I am a genuine bastard. My mother reared me by herself in her Auntie's brothel.'

'He always looks and sounds good, doesn't he?' John observed, 'but then you're trained to look after him, aren't you?'

The familiarity of Steve and his behaviour was never examined any further than a feeling because between Gemma, pregnancy, work, trying to keep writing and staying one step ahead of disaster left me too tired to think about anything very much. There was always later.

Trisha and Don offered to take Gemma for a while to give me a break. They couldn't have children of their own. I was desperately sorry for them but Gemma was my daughter not theirs. They turned on me telling me I was self-centered and selfish, pumping out kids willy-nilly with no way of looking after them. At least not as well as they could in their opinion. I made a bet with myself that I had more in the bank than they did. I didn't spend mine on keeping up appearances but Gemma was just as hooked into them as I was entangled in Steve.

As the pregnancy wore on I found it more and more difficult to recognise myself. I kept up the pretence that everything was fine, in part to protect Gemma and insanely enough, Steve's budding career and public image. It was beginning to bloom at the expense of mine. Mine had been absorbed into his. It seemed all the traits I thought I had, being independent, able to stand on my own two feet, a career as a writer taking off were being used very cleverly against me. Or maybe I never had them in the first place. I was being filtered through Steve and he handed me back to me with everything of value stripped from me. I looked the same but the only meaning I had was what he gave me.

A few weeks before Rosie was born I'd come home from work then fallen asleep on the sofa. I woke to find Steve kneeling beside me gently stroking my hair. Several people watched him from the doorway, smiling at his affectionate display. Steve was on his way out with them.

'You revolt me,' he whispered in my ear. 'You're revolting. You look like a big fat ugly slug. You make me sick.' With each kiss on my cheek he hurt me harder. 'Big. Fat. Slug. Pig.'

From a distance it would've looked as if he was almost worshipping me. He gave me a last hard kiss on my lips before he got up. Gemma climbed into bed and hugged me. From childhood I knew the more reactions you gave the greater the punishment and the more they gloated. I didn't want to upset Gemma either so I began to plan my escape but I hadn't factored in Rosie being sick from the minute she was born.

The night I went into labour Steve told me I was putting it on because I didn't want him to go out. I picked up the phone to ring Philippe to babysit Gemma but Steve cut the phone call off. He was stoned again. We got to the hospital courtesy of a lift from one of our neighbours. I had Rosie within fifteen minutes without fear, without panic, without pain. When she was born her cry told me there was something wrong with her. She sounded as if she had damage to her brain. No-one else could hear it. Her cry was too high-pitched. I'd paid for a private room and my own doctor months beforehand. Although the doctor turned up in a blue ball gown after the delivery I didn't get the privacy I paid for.

Steve held Rosie for a couple of seconds before he told me he'd take Gemma home and put her to bed.

As he walked past the nurse's station I heard him tell the staff he wasn't married to me, I wasn't married to anybody and I had no idea who Gemma's father was. He also believed that Rosie was not his. He strolled out.

His information triggered Rosie's removal from me. I demanded her back. A nurse came around to give me an injection. I asked her what was in it. She told me it was none of my business. I told her I didn't want it. She called for another nurse to come and help her. They injected me with what I assumed was a sleeping mixture. Most things acted in the opposite way they were meant to on me. On speed I spent the next hour with my finger on the buzzer demanding Rosie back. I was dressed and ready to go by the time I got her back.

Philippe and John had responded to my phone call to come to the hospital as a matter of urgency. They took me home and put me to bed. The next-door neighbour was minding Gemma because Steve'd decided to go out after all.

'Do you want me to have a word with him?' Philippe asked as John held the baby while I placed Gemma on my lap and held her tightly.

Dad used to use that phrase too.

'No. I'm going to change the locks.'

Philippe and John stayed the rest of the night and made breakfast for Gemma and me. Rosie was sick on my breast milk so I fed her some cooled boiled water in a bottle. She was very distressed and there was nothing much I could do to calm her. Gemma'd decided to hate her. Steve came back around two the next afternoon just as John and Philippe were on their way home.

'Oh you're back,' was all he said. He went to the refrigerator and pulled out a lettuce.

He began nibbling on the leaves.

John watched him for a while before he spoke.

'So you eat like a rabbit too?'

Steve looked at him blankly then went to make himself some coffee. John quizzed Steve.

'Why did you tell the hospital staff that Jenny was a single parent?'

Steve looked stricken.

'Did it cause trouble?'

He put his arm around me, tears in his eyes.

'I'm so sorry. They asked me if we were married and I said no.'

Philippe and John checked with me for the truth.

'I heard the whole thing. They did not ask you. You volunteered the information.'

Steve shrugged and went into the bedroom and closed the door.

John broke the silence.

'You need to be very careful of him.'

'Better still,' Philippe looked darkly towards the bedroom door, 'get rid of him as soon as you can. He hates you.'

Vaguely through the tiredness came the thought that if Steve'd succeeded I would've lost both children last night. Rosie's crying distracted me. To my consternation she was sick again on my breast milk.

The roller coaster began.

The chemist sold me baby formula. It made her sicker and all the substitute milks made her break out in a rash. She went into anaphylaxis on cow's milk. She screamed day and night. Steve left. He'd found a red-haired flautist who thought he was a wonderful accompaniment to her sound. She let him sleep day and night at her place until he became too expensive. Next was a schoolteacher. He showed the kids at her school how to play guitar. With this new slew of women he rarely turned up but, just in case, I kept my money in my pockets just in case.

Despite my taking an enormous amount of time preparing Gemma for the baby she was beside herself with jealousy and fought Rosie for attention. I was woken from a five-minute coma-like sleep one morning by loud thumping.

'Wait. Wait,' Gemma yelled in the distance. 'You forgot something.'

I raced outside to find her dragging Rosie, blankets and all down the footpath to dump her in the garbage truck. I picked Rosie up and took Gemma's hand with the other. I'd have to make more time for her, starting with hiding the nail scissors so she couldn't cut Rosie's hair off again.

I decided to ignore Steve and just concentrate on the kids. The beginning of my long journey around the medical fraternity to try to find someone to help me with Rosie took up all my time. She couldn't keep any food down, her skin was red raw and she was having epileptic fits that lasted what seemed for hours. She was blue and grey and frothing. Barley water soothed her but her food intake was alarmingly small.

One doctor said it was my fault for having a short labour. I should've been made stop it and behave myself.

"Perhaps I should've put a stick between my teeth," I'd said.

My answering back proved I couldn't behave myself so I didn't deserve medical help. The next said she'd grow out of it. Rosie was just attention-seeking. Well you would if you were two weeks old and starving wouldn't you?

Another doctor gave me a can of powdered soy milk.

After drinking it, everywhere Rosie's urine splashed it burnt the skin off her tiny body. When she did sleep it was in second-long catnaps. The rest of the time she screamed. The doctor reacted in fury at my reporting that Rosie appeared to be unable to tolerate soy milk. He took it as a personal insult. He began to throw cans of soymilk at me as he ordered me out of his office. No one was allergic to soy milk he screamed. I was making it all up. With Rosie in one arm and Gemma holding my hand I twisted my body this way and that to stop them being hit by the cans. Gemma was terrified.

Steve refused to come to doctor's appointments with me.

'You're on your own,' he said. 'I'm getting married. We're going to America. She's got contacts there to help me with my career.'

Rosie was less than a month old.

In a vague haze I'd heard a recommendation for a paediatrician in Melbourne. John knew someone who had a house for rent there. I paid for the first month. I had to get help for Rosie before she died of starvation. She couldn't hold any food down. Philippe and John agreed to come down to see me once I'd settled in.

On the day of my departure Steve had come back together with his girlfriend. They and her friends were in the lounge room. All of them were so involved in the unfolding drama between Steve and his girlfriend and what he was going to do about me I was completely ignored. After I booked a taxi I walked into the lounge room to pick Gemma up from Steve's lap. His fiancé was wearing my beautiful Burmese peridot green-gold ring on her finger. I'd come home from my fruitless search for help in the medical profession when Steve'd told me someone had broken in and stolen all my jewellery, other valuables I had and various presents I'd been given for Rosie. He'd told the police he said. I didn't bother to check. I knew he hadn't. Steve's fiancé was screaming at him to make up his mind about whether he was going to stay with me or marry her.

I took Gemma by the hand and walked outside. The taxi driver waited patiently while I strapped the children in and put my possessions in the boot. Philippe, John and Odette had helped me pack the big stuff and send it ahead a few days beforehand. It should be waiting for me when I got there. The rest could be left behind with Steve and his new girlfriend. She was already dressed in some of my clothes. I checked I still had my transistor radio in my jacket then the taxi drove away.

We went to Central Station, got on the train and within minutes we were gone.

JEREMIAH

The dog was biting through the cage wire in the pound when we approached. All around him other dogs were howling or clawing at the cage, desperate for someone to let them out. He appraised us quickly with large brown liquid eyes before he returned to concentrate on his breakout. Gemma put her small hand out to touch his black nose and pat him on it. He stopped what he was doing and smiled at her.

The attendant saw us still standing by the cage.

'He's a cross between an Alsatian and a Daschund.'

She was almost apologising for his low–strung brown appearance.

'What sort of dog are you looking for?'

'One that's a bit more reliable than a bloke.'

The area I was renting in appeared very run down and rather seedy. I thought a dog might be more useful and a better fit in our family. When the attendant opened the cage to let the dog out he made no attempt to escape. Instead he came to stand by my side and then began to carefully check us out by smelling us thoroughly first. The kids adored him on sight.

'I think he likes you.'

The attendant slipped a lead on him and I took him home.

Once inside I took the lead off but again he didn't try to leave. He went over to the children and stood guard. I turned my radio on so the dog felt more at home. When the postman tried to deliver mail through the door, the dog just about took his hand off. We decided to call him Jeremiah, after the bullfrog Gemma liked to sing about. He became Jerry for short. I dimly remembered from bible studies long ago what the first Jeremiah had said his gods had told him once: Attack you they will, overcome you they can't.

We hadn't been there long when half a dozen children turned up at my front door to beg me for food. After I fed them we walked them home. They lived in the falling down, unpainted house with unkempt grounds on the corner. I'd thought it had been abandoned.

Their mother was a tiny woman, beaten black and blue. She seemed to have shrivelled into a shrunken life that trembled uncontrollably at the front door. She told me her husband would be in jail for the next ten years but his mates paid the rent and bought the food for her and the kids. This week they'd decided she could live on white bread and tomato sauce because she had broken one of the rules her husband had laid down for her to follow. She didn't know which one. His mates had belted her up on his behalf to pull her into line.

'The children are desperately hungry,' she whispered.

I dropped food over her fence whenever I could; sometimes I'd fasten money to a tin with a rubber band hoping like hell I wasn't seen. I didn't want to make her situation worse. Or mine.

The doctor's appointment finally rolled around. I explained to her that Rosie had gone into anaphylaxis with cow's milk and she appeared to be allergic to most foodstuffs. I was desperate as she was covered in a rash, was not gaining weight and I thought she'd die if I couldn't get food down her neck. She screamed in agony day and night from the food I tried to feed her until she was able to get rid of it out of her body. I'd begun to hallucinate from lack of sleep. I felt helpless and beyond exhausted. It was all my fault because I had a massive amount of allergies and I must have given them to Rosie but Gemma was alright.

The doctor admitted Rosie to the children's hospital. My money ebbed away on tests and extras. Rosie had been there several days when I was called back into the doctor's office. She told me Rosie was being discharged from the hospital immediately. I protested, saying that her test results had not come back and nothing had been resolved. The doctor told me I was not welcome at the hospital and Rosie would never be admitted there again.

In disbelief I listened as she told me Steve had turned up with his drug addict mates on the pretext of visiting Rosie as the concerned father. They'd broken into the nurses' station to steal syringes and drugs. I didn't know he was in Melbourne. I told the doctor that I was very sorry but it was neither Rosie's fault nor mine. I had left Steve. He had not signed Rosie's birth certificate and he'd told me he never would because he didn't have to. Paternity was his word against mine. As we weren't married and he denied he was Rosie's father, I argued, it should've been enough legal grounds to keep him away from the hospital. The doctor called security to escort us from the hospital.

When I contacted Philippe he told me that Trisha and Don had given Steve all my information. They felt sorry for him as his wedding plans hadn't worked out because he said he couldn't get over me. John assumed what he couldn't get over was he had to get a job and pay for his own board and lodgings for once.

I decided to look at Rosie as if she were a landscape. I'd search for answers to the problems in her. I drew up lists of what she could eat and what she couldn't to see if there was a pattern. Later I went for a walk with the kids and the dog while I tried to clear my head. I went over and over my finances trying to calculate how long I could last without work.

At the park Jerry defined a boundary and neither the children nor anyone else was allowed to cross it. Freshly roasted and ground coffee scented the air. We wandered over to it.

The Greek owners made a giant fuss of Gemma and gave her Milo with a marshmallow on top. While I waited for the coffee I looked around at what the shop stocked. Although she was allergic to every other form of milk, I hadn't tried Rosie on sheep or goat's milk products. I didn't know it existed. Even though I'd been reared on mutton I'd never thought of milking a sheep. The Greek owners gave me a glass of goat's milk and a teaspoon to feed Rosie. She gorged it down. I waited for her to die on it. She wanted more.

I mashed up some sheep's milk cheese with my fingers and let her suck it off my fingers. I finally had something to feed her on that didn't make her sick. Slowly Rosie began to gain weight and together we built up her food repertoire. Steve made no effort to contact me. I could think again but out of nowhere an abscess formed on my back tooth and it nearly felled me.

Mum rang in between my phoning dentists for an emergency appointment that was a day or so away. I can't remember why she rang. It think it was because they'd had some rain and Dad was getting offers for the property and they could go back to Brisbane at last. She said she would come down to help me.

I'd only met this woman once or twice before. After giving me a bright kiss on my forehead it seemed at the same time she put a load of washing on and made lunch. She played with the children, read stories and danced and sang with them. She looked after me once the tooth was pulled out. When the swelling went down on my face she took me out to buy me new clothes in size ten. I was dressed in black velvet trousers with a pale pink top and black high-heeled boots.

She was everything I had ever wanted in a mother. She told me Steve only saw me as a meal ticket and I could do without him. She was very sure I'd survive this rough patch and make it in life. I could see the woman Dad'd fallen in love with. I fell in love with her too. We had nearly a week of wonder together before the phone rang.

Baby Girl had put her foot down on the accelerator of her car and, at high speed, had driven it into a brick wall. In an instant my mother disappeared and Mum was back in her place. Without a word she packed her things and left. I rang Jake. She was inconsolable. Baby Girl had been out droving with Dad and Young Tom and everything seemed to be okay. I suspected Amanda was behind it.

In the psychiatric ward the doctors were questioning Mum and Dad about Baby Girl's suicide attempts. They demanded to know why she dressed and acted like a man. Mum was furious. She was not going to be questioned or held to account by anybody. She contacted every relative she had and Baby Girl was soon discharged. She was back out on the property away from everyone. No one would know our business, no one at all. Mum, Dad and Amanda formed a wall around Baby Girl that was impenetrable.

When I rang to speak to Baby Girl, Amanda'd hissed down the phone, 'Slut. Slut. Slut. Slut. Slut—'until I hung up.

Jake wasn't allowed to see her either. Lincoln was up on country again and I couldn't get hold of him. Baby Girl was on her own.

One morning Jerry began to bark and growl wildly at the front door. This was different from his monstering the postman performance. His growl was deep back in his throat and his teeth were bared. I held onto his collar before I opened the door. A burly man was knifing the black and blue woman with a butcher's knife on my doorstep. Her children were outside the fence watching silent and white-faced. When the burly man held up the knife to plunge it into her chest again I let Jerry's collar go. He sprang into the air, locked his jaws around the man's knife wrist and brought him to the ground. I stamped my boot as hard as I could on the man's elbow to break it. After it smashed I kicked the knife away. My front porch was covered in blood and profanities. Without turning, I told Gemma to go back to the lounge room and stay there.

I watched as neighbours came running, not to help us, but to pick up the woman and carry her away to a waiting car. Some men assisted the knife man down the street. Another came to retrieve the knife. I held Jerry's collar again. He was all I had between them and me. Further up the street I saw the black and blue woman's children being shoved into another car. Several more men turned up. A tall one with spiffy blonde hair held up with a jar of Brylcreem plugged in a garden hose. A bald man with a Friar Tuck fringe began to sweep with a straw broom as the other sprayed the porch with water. They washed the blood and any other evidence away.

Shortly afterwards another man in a dark blue expensive Italian silk suit, a candy striped pink and blue tie and a natty hat came daintily up the path.

'Nice little kiddies you have. You wouldn't want anything to happen to them.'

Jerry wanted to rip pieces out of them on our behalf. It was all I could do to hold onto him. I stared the natty man down for a very long time, then went inside and shut the door.

"If anyone asks," I could hear Dad say. "You tell them nothink. You never go to the coppers even if you're on your last legs."

I moved from St Kilda as soon as I could.

When she was twelve months old, Rosie was diagnosed with autism. I was advised to put her into an institution and leave her there.

"Have another one," the consultant said as if Rosie was a defunct toaster and a replacement'd make up for it.

Later as Rosie pulled out the one coloured building block that brought down the edifice Gemma had build, the diagnosis was changed to high-functioning autistic. It required a great deal of thought to pick out that block. My heart soared with hope.

In our new suburb Gemma'd attached herself to a small group of children being taken for a walk. They were part of a wonderful playgroup run by Mrs. Peart. The kids adored her. Peart'd told me Gemma was most welcome to join the group for a small fee but when I told her Rosie was a high-functioning autistic she wouldn't take her. She gave me the name of another group several suburbs away.

"Most bovine woman I've ever come across," Peart told me. "Put her there dear. Let her copy the other kids. She'll learn that way."

Going on instinct and responding to Rosie's cues Gemma and I used flash cards, movement, dance, exercise, swings, music—anything to get her to respond and to keep her stimulated. At her nursery the bovine owner put her with her best normal children so Rosie could copy their behaviour. With both children in day care I grabbed the first menial job I could. I was almost broke.

I could obey the rules for rail transport when I wasn't working but now that I had to go to work they proved to be an obstacle for working women but not for working men. Despite the fact I'd paid for an adult weekly ticket, the stationmaster'd informed me that the old rules still applied. I wasn't allowed on the train or any public transport for that matter until after nine-thirty in the morning. I could carry Rosie onto the train before seven to take her to the nursery or after nine-thirty but I had to pick her up before three or else leave her until six-thirty in the evening. No pram or stroller could be used. Public transport was for the working man and they didn't want to be inconvenienced by women with children.

Men were the only people who peed as well. As most women's toilets were closed when I wanted to take the kids to them I had no qualms about taking them to the men's. Women who missed the public transport curfews sat on the platforms and cried from exhaustion. While Gemma went to a six o'clock breakfast with Peart I stood in the guard's carriage before seven then carried Rosie to the nursery. I ran back to the station to travel to work before I repeated it all later in the afternoon. Most times I was so tired all I could do was feed the children, hug them and tell them how much I loved them.

The atmosphere around me began to darken but I put it down to nursing very heavy, incontinent, geriatric patients eight hours a day to the point of exhaustion. One afternoon after I finished my day shift I began to run towards the station when Rupert grabbed me by my arm.

'I always know where you are.'

He laughed as he gripped my arm tighter.

'You can't escape me.'

As if it were a joke.

'I went to your old place. Steve'd told me you were there. I didn't know you'd moved. The neighbours said Steve'd been there for a couple of days. Just lying on the front porch. It took me a while to find you. You'd better go and see if he's alright. He's been a good friend to me.'

'No.'

Rupert wouldn't let my arm go.

'If you're so worried about him, you look after him. Steve is a liar, a thief and a cheat. There's nothing wrong with him. Get one of his girlfriends to take him in. I have to pick up my daughter and get home.'

Rupert twisted my arm up my back.

'If I can't have you then he can. I won't stand for you whoring yourself around from bloke to bloke. You need to stick to one bloke and that's him.'

He shoved me into his car.

'You're going to look after him and you and I are going to get him right now.'

We picked up Rosie then drove to St Kilda. On the way Rupert told me his marriage had ended. He was planning to kill his wife and children then himself.

Steve was lying on the front verandah like a small smelly starfish. The only thing he was going to die of was drama. Rupert went over to get him then put him in the back seat of the car. Rosie began rocking frantically when she saw him. Rupert drove us back to my townhouse.

'You're home, buddy. She'll look after you from now on.'

Gemma was overjoyed to see Steve again. Rosie wouldn't go near him. Steve recovered almost immediately and took up exactly where he left off. He trashed my life for no other reason that he could. I'd given up having women friends because Steve propositioned them all or made their life such hell they stayed away from me.

He used Rosie and her fear of him to keep her on edge and in screaming bouts so I had no quiet or time to myself. Shortly after he came back he began to fake illnesses again. Asthma attacks were now his specialty. Every time I told him to leave he'd either promise to change or have an attack. They came on at night when he'd packed his bag and taken it to the front door. After six o'clock I had to pay for a doctor to come to attend to him.

One doctor I'd called several times in one night told me Steve wasn't even trying to respond to medication. He thought Steve was faking and I had difficulty throwing a sick person out on the street. When I tried to reason with him he'd shrug and say, "If you don't like it then you should be stricter with me." As if he was a naughty little boy who kept showing all the other kids at kindie his penis.

Hugely over-extended my body was just about as broken as my mind. "I'm not your mother," I'd reply.

The over-all threat was that Rupert'd come back again to see how his best mate, Steve was getting on. My life was in free-fall. It felt as if it was happening to someone else. I kept Rosie in childcare from the time she woke until she went to sleep and Gemma stayed down with Peart until dark. It would limit their contact with Steve to about thirty minutes.

One of my neighbours came to ask me if I had a spare room as a friend of his needed one for a while.

Frankie turned up. She'd named herself after Frank Sinatra, her singing idol. She was blonde, blue eyed, sassy, tall and athletic. I liked her immediately. I knew she'd have no problems handling Steve. I gave her his room. She told me she'd conduct her business away from the townhouse. One night Steve returned after an absence of a few weeks. Frankie introduced herself to him. Later I heard several loud thumps.

'Do you want this bum here, Jen?' she called out to me.

'No,' I yelled back down the stairs.

Frankie black-belted him all the way to the footpath.

With her as my lifeline I tried to get my squalid, sordid life back on track. Frankie'd take the kids shopping and to the hairdressing salons she used so I could sleep or catch up on the housework. The kids'd return home dressed in black velvet with hair piled high on their heads. We dined out at reasonably expensive restaurants and laughed a lot. She bought me an Aretha Franklin record for my birthday. Life was slowly turning to normal. By the time Frankie fell in love with one of her clients and they decided to move in together, I felt strong enough to cope on my own again.

While the children were asleep I tentatively touched the piano. I picked up my pen and walked over to the big easy chair.

The phone rang.

A nurse from a psychiatric hospital demanded I rescue Steve immediately. If I didn't he would die within the next twenty-four hours.

'Rescue him yourself.'

"I can't. I work here."

'Isn't it your job?'

'His liver has failed. He hasn't eaten for days.'

'Did you tell him the food was free? That he didn't have to pay for it?'

'He put you down as his next of kin.'

'I bet he did.'

I hung up the phone and took it off the hook for the night. I figured if he knew I wasn't coming he'd get himself out of any mess he was in or get someone else to do it for him.

I began writing just some song lyrics to start with. They were desperately sad in a bluesy kind of way. The next afternoon the phone rang again with the same plea. After several days, fed up, I got the next-door-neighbour to mind the children while I went to the hospital.

A male nurse stood on the other side of the locked door. He was shouting it wasn't visiting hours. I held on tightly to the doorknob as I pretended I couldn't hear him. He finally unlocked the door and as he did so, I pulled the door towards me and then slammed it back, knocking him to the floor.

I strode into the ward. I was going to tell Steve the jig was up. No one believed his lies anymore and he could get out of the bloody bed, get a job and leave us alone except his skin was bright yellow and he looked like he was in a coma.

I locked his arm around mine.

'Don't let go.'

The nursing staff came running in.

'Get an ambulance.'

'We tried to feed him but he refused.'

It must have been the first time in his life Steve'd knocked back a free feed.

'Get an ambulance.'

'What's he got against us?'

'Get an ambulance.'

Two ambulance officers took Steve to the hospital.

I gave his parents' details as his next-of-kin and left. His mother made it perfectly clear she didn't want him. He'd caused nothing but trouble and grief in her household she yelled at me, so why would she want it back again? His father said Steve was probably bunging it all on and he couldn't be bothered coming down to see it or, in case it was true, to say goodbye. He'd had enough.

Steve recovered.

At the front door he burst into tears when Gemma flung herself around him. Rosie remained more cautious. I picked up my purse and slung it over my shoulder so it stayed under my arm. Steve told me he'd changed his ways. He was going to go to therapy.

'As long as I don't have to pay for it I don't care.'

He told me he wanted to move back in. I refused and went to close the door. He grabbed my hair and twisted it around in his fingers as he shoved me inside. He began to smack my head into the kitchen table. Gemma ran to get our next-door neighbours. By the time they came Steve appeared to be stark raving mad in the Germanic manner of early celluloid. He wouldn't let my hair go but I had the feeling he was using madness to covertly bash me to punish me for not letting him stay.

With Steve ripping the hair out of my head we took him back to the hospital to re-admit him. As Steve sat in the office chair looking like a classic movie madman I told the psychiatrist I thought Steve was having him on. He was expert at putting on sicknesses to get his own way.

The psychiatrist was horrified by my attitude. He told me that I'd caused Steve's mental illness because I had emasculated him by assuming the traditional male role. Steve was left with no meaning in his life or purpose because I had usurped it.

Steve peeped from under his adorable fluffy fringe to see how it was all going.

'If you would just stay at home and be a normal woman undertaking the duties of a suburban housewife and allow Steve to be the breadwinner then he would not be as sick as he is. I now doubt he will ever be released from hospital again,' the psychiatrist concluded his Freudian misogynist rant with a flourish.

At that moment Steve jumped up on the doctor's desk and kicked everything from it. Two male nurses ran in and restrained him.

Steve smirked at me.

'I'm sorry he's de-balled and all,' I drawled, 'but we've got to eat.'

I wearily got to my feet.

'Enjoy the rest of your life, Steve. Looks like fun.'

He signed himself out the next day.

Another woman had come to save him from the hospital and me. The psychiatrist was furious with Steve's miraculous recovery. He told me Steve, with his history of lying, manipulation, womanising, theft, mother-hatred, drug taking and faking illnesses was probably a psychopath.

I didn't know what that really meant nor did I understand why I had landed up with one. I could no longer tell who or what I was anymore let alone work out what anyone else was doing.

After an absence of several months Steve came to see me. He was very contrite. He wanted to be more involved with the children. He loved me more than life itself and he wanted to come back. He'd change.

Translation from Steve-speak to plain English told me his

relationship with other women was over temporarily and he had nowhere else to go. Gemma desperately wanted him home. I was lost in the wasteland of my own life. In order to have anything I had to get rid of Steve permanently. He wouldn't go for as long as he thought I had money or any creative energy he could suck out of me to prop up his pretence at artistic ambitions. His art wasn't being used to make money. It was being used to snooker women. I had to stop him hooking into me.

The invisible threads of I love you, I will change or the children want me around had to be broken forever. Once there was absolutely nothing left for him to take he'd find someone or something with better prospects than me. Meantime I'd continue with backbreaking menial work to support us all.

The long farewell began when Steve announced he wanted to go to Perth to further his career. I knew it was a Steve-speak for he'd found another woman and he didn't have the money to meet up with her. I had to pay for it by selling everything I had. He wouldn't go unless I came with him. I knew he wanted me to be completely and utterly destitute if not dead so that he had triumphed over his mother.

The neighbours'd send Jerry over after I got to Perth. The children didn't want to be without him. I told Philippe and John I'd see them soon.

Once in Perth I waited for the right moment.

It came from an unexpected quarter.

I grabbed it with both hands and held on.

TRAVELLIN'

It was as if I'd blundered around in the dark all my life when a Labor Party politician from the Cabramatta district in Sydney's western suburbs called Gough Whitlam switched on the lights. He told us it was time. Time for freedom. Time to move. Time to begin. Time to sweep the Menzies' cohort and their cronies out of power. Time had brought change.

Whitlam's Labor Party swept into power and began what the Murdoch media screamed in bold type was a mindless revolution that would ruin the country and everyone in it.

Within weeks Whitlam and the Labor Party eliminated conscription and criminal execution. They brought in free universal health-care, free University education, legal aid programs, encouraged tourism to Australia, set up a new city at Albury-Wodonga, standardised rail gauges, built roads, instituted urban renewal in our decaying cities and sewered them. Whitlam's activities fueled the fires of resentment in his foes who had not managed to lift the standard of living in Australia by any design or plan, except for themselves, since the nineteen twenties. Australians were always going to share in the good life but not yet.

The 'First Among Equals' were so enraged at being dumped from government and so unable to comprehend or accept its defeat, they immediately began to plot to seize government back again by fair means or foul.

Menzies' Liberal-Country Party, the Coalition, were sure their dim-witted Australian public had made a mistake by voting them out after twenty-odd years. All they had to do was point out the error of its ways to them and they'd restore them to government again. They were also sure it'd only take a few months to bring the Labor Government down. The Murdoch media began to drip-feed virulent anti-Whitlam economic horror stories and salacious scandals to the public.

The 'right one' Steve had waiting for him on the platform in Perth turned out to be wrong. Within my hearing he'd told her he'd had to con me into buying the tickets because he had no money. It wasn't his best pickup line because she left him on the platform.

After I got a job day nursing I concentrated on making life for the children the best it could be and the happiest while I waited for Steve to leave. We almost had nothing left. I wanted the kids to grow in as peaceful a home as I could muster. I'd tied myself to the mast of my tiny boat so I couldn't end up back with him again. My lack of reaction to his sound was because of the beeswax I plugged into my ears so I wouldn't hear his siren songs.

Gemma loved her new school and skipped and sang there and back. Rosie was thriving and loved kindie. She'd come out of most of her autistic behaviour as a warm and funny little kid who still did everything literally. I learned not to say "Pull up your socks" when I meant she was to keep her room tidy. Perfume and lights still made her muddled but we figured out alternatives. She danced and sang to the Abba songs Gemma strummed on her ukulele.

Change was blowing in on the north-westerly winds but Gough Whitlam and I both knew we would not be allowed to live how we wanted for too long. We both had to work as fast as we could to change the world around us before the doors shut onus again. It was time. Time to move things along.

'Steve? I'm going to start writing tomorrow.'

Steve came into the kitchen looking puzzled and a bit annoyed. He'd thought all that nonsense was over.

'I want you to take the children out for the morning so I can write.'

'Your mother doesn't want you around,' Steve declared loudly to the children over Sunday breakfast. 'So I'm taking you down to the park.'

Earth shattering screams rent the air.

'Why don't you want us anymore? What have we done? We don't want to go to the park. We want to stay here.'

The children clung onto me in desperation. The dog joined in. Steve was more than pleased with their reaction. It was designed to shatter my nerves and my resolve. I looked at the children. I had to do it. I had to.

Steve dragged the children sobbing and crying out of the house. The dog stayed behind to keep me company. I refused to feel guilty despite his accusing liquid brown eyes.

I re-established order by making the beds. I put the china and plastic breakfast things in the sink and wiped down the table. I washed up, made a cup of tea, lit a cigarette and tried to calm myself down.

I got out my lipstick red portable typewriter and wound some paper into it. I began to type the opening lines of what I hoped would be my first novel: I wish I co—

And they were back.

'Well what have you written?'

Steve leaned over my shoulder to read the words on the paper.

'Is that it? Three and a half words? What's the point of me taking the kids and putting up with all their shit if that's all you're going to do? You've wasted my time and now I'm running late. I've got to meet people for coffee.'

He took money out of my purse and whistling a song he walked out.

The kids began to climb on me again. The dog had his paws on my leg. I wondered why I expected better behaviour from Steve after all this time.

The next morning while the kids and Steve were eating breakfast I whacked the typewriter on the table where my breakfast plate should've been.

I typed up the rest of the sentence I'd been forced to abandon the day before: — uld see it. Mum wrote the other day—

And Steve slammed his chair against the table and walked out.

The children stopped eating waiting to see what I'd do. I continued to type as if nothing had happened. The kids resumed eating. The dog curled around my feet. No matter what happened I was going to write. I'd continue to write about anything and everything that happened around me.

It'd been a long, long time.

My short story was accepted for broadcast on the national radio broadcaster, the ABC.

Now all I had to do was wait until Steve played out his end game.

While Gough Whitlam worked as fast as he could to change the face of Australia before Menzies' 'First among Equals' cohort threw him out, I did the same.

Everything was packed.

Everything was in place.

It was just a matter of time.

A CONVERSATION WITH RITA

Her car chugged along the road and hid around the corner. The children got out of it then ran towards the house. Steve came up to the front door behind them. I hoped he didn't notice my purse tucked tightly under my arm. The kids hung back a bit. I smiled as I tried to speak as calmly as I could.

'Steve? Would you take the kids inside for me please?'

'I can't stay you know.'

Steve's reply was a little too cocky.

'I want to talk to you—and Rita.'

'What about?'

'I think it's time we talked. I'd like to invite her inside for coffee.'

'You kids go inside. I'll be there in a minute—when I've finished talking to your mother.'

'Go on kids.' I bent down to give each of them a kiss as I ushered them inside. 'We'll be there in a minute. Get ready for bed.'

The kids held hands as they walked towards the bedroom. They glanced back before they disappeared from sight.

'What do you want to talk about—with Rita and me?'

'I think we need to sort things out.'

'We don't have time right now.'

'Steve, this can't go on. I think it's time we talked ok?'

'I don't want you to say anything to upset her.'

'I won't.'

'I'll get her. She'll freak out if she sees you. She's very sensitive.'

'Oh right. Would you mind? I'd rather ask her myself. Could you go inside and look after the children? Put them to bed for me?'

'No. I'll wait here—just to keep an eye on things.'

'I'll be back in a minute.'

I've been cast as the mad woman in a medieval melodrama.

Rabid, maddened, furious, possessed, frantic, demented,

uncontrollable, berserk – she crawled cunningly to the car, ripped the door open and clutching Rita in her teeth, snarled her way across the paddock. Steve leapt to his horse. In the fading light, Steve was shocked and horrified to find his wife raving, rambling, incoherent (and sick) in the back paddock. The only thing left of his beloved Rita was a few blonde hairs floating wispily around the blubbering lips of what was once his wife (and the mother of his two children). Slowly, Steve raised his rifle.

'Hello, Rita. I'm Jenny. Steve's former partner.'

Or whatever I was.

'I want to apologise for my behaviour over the past couple of weeks. I haven't been —.'

Co-operative?

'There's no need to apologise, Jenny. I understand.'

'Would you like to come inside, Rita? I'd like to talk to you and Steve, if you don't mind.'

A few weeks ago Steve'd asked me if I wanted to go see a play. A friend of his in the new band had given him some free tickets.

'Is Steve ok with it?'

'Of course.'

Steve'd told me that he'd felt guilty about neglecting me and the kids but he'd wanted to make it up to me. That's why he wanted to take me to the play. We didn't see enough of each other because I worked all night in nursing homes and he was getting another band together during the day. He was sorry about the way he'd behaved over my getting my stories broadcast. I went along with the charade.

I tried to have a conversation with Rita.

'I realise that things mustn't have been too good for you lately –.'

Steve'd even organised a babysitter so we could go to the theatre: Roger, the guitar player.

I'd been a bit apprehensive about leaving Roger to babysit but Steve'd told me that he had experience with children. His wife was pregnant. He took me to a play put on by some students at The Tech.

Rita and I approached the house.

'Just be careful on that step Rita. It's loose.'

Steve called out from the kids' bedroom.

'Rita? Will you be alright by yourself for a few minutes?'

'Yeah, sure.'

She smiled lovingly towards the bedroom.

We'd been the only ones in the theatre. I'd gone to sit in the middle of it but Steve'd other ideas.

'I'll be out as soon as I've finished reading the kids a story, honey.'

'Let's sit in the kitchen, Rita. It's warmer there.'

'Go right up the front, Jen,' Steve'd said as we'd stood in the aisle of the empty theatre. 'You bag two seats while I get the program. I'd rather sit right up the front. You can see better. Would you like some coffee?'

After I'd given him the money to pay for it I'd wandered up the front. No doubt it was going to be a cracker of a performance.

I filled the jug with water.

'Would you like some coffee?'

A few more people'd come into the theatre and sat down. Steve'd gone over to chat to them before he came back to join me. The play'd begun.

"These actors are shit hot, aren't they, Jen?" Steve'd said in a theatrical whisper as he'd nudged me. "You'd never know they were only first year students would you?"

Rita pulled a chair out and sat down near my typewriter.

'I'd rather wait for Steve to come to see what he's having. Thanks.'

Steve'd continued talking to me as he pointed actors out for special mention. "I think the one playing the part of Mary is fantastic, Jen, don't you?" And he'd laughed.

'Steve told me you thought I over-acted.'

Of course he did.

'That's cool. I can take criticism.'

She flicked her long blonde hair out of the way.

After the curtain closed I'd turned to Steve. "We ought to go backstage to thank the person who gave us the tickets. It'd felt really good to go out somewhere again without the kids."

Steve'd panicked. He'd told me he hated going backstage. I laughed at him and said, "Don't be silly. We live backstage." It was deserted when we got there. Steve'd wanted to get a cab home.

'I don't know much about Lillian Hellmann. Is that the first play you've done? I mean, of hers?'

'*The Children's Hour* is one of her better known ones. She's having a revival of sorts in the States because of the Democrats and stuff.'

Rita sounded rather bored.

When we'd come home Roger'd told us the children were no problem and he'd run. Steve'd taken me in his arms and told me he'd never loved or wanted me so much in all his life.

'Steve's coming. I'll put the kettle on again. This has gone cold.'

'I hope you don't think that we took you to the play because—.'

She stopped as if to consider for the first time what light her behaviour might've cast her in.

The next morning Steve was still in bed. By midday I'd already prepared a chicken for lunch. I'd called out to him, asking him to get up and get dressed as we were all starving.

Rita continued to explain herself.

'We just thought you needed to go out somewhere.'

Steve'd come to the table in his underpants. I'd asked him if he wanted the leg or the wing.

'We didn't mean to embarrass you or anything.'

I'd put the leg on the plate for Steve. He'd shoved my typewriter out of the way. Half way through eating he'd stopped to ask me if I remembered the girl in the play from the previous night, the one with the blonde hair who played Mary? I'd steeled myself. "Well we're in love," he said as he poured some gravy on his potatoes.

No matter how much you prepare for it, it still takes your breath away.

Rita warmed up in conversation with me.

'I'm finding the music scene really exciting, you know. It must've been fantastic for you all those years, Jenny. There's so much—it's really different from theatre—really great energy floating around. I'm doing backup vocals for Steve which is such fun. He's going to be really big, a star. Pete says in a few months he'll have at least a number one, if not an album full of hits. Everyone I've met so far seems so—I don't know—creative—free. You know?'

That Sunday I'd kept carving the chicken and allotted portions to the children's plates and then cut the food up for them.

"I'll go as soon as I've finished lunch," Steve'd said as he'd helped himself to seconds.

"You can't."

"Why?"

"I've taken all your clothes to the laundromat."

'Would you like some toast, Rita?'

I walked over to the cupboard to get the bread out then put a few slices in the toaster.

'Thanks. Steve told me you were a feminist. I've never seen the point of it myself.'

'Really? I would have thought if anything I was an advocate of human rights as well. One slice or two?'

Steve'd waited while I got dessert. He'd told me he'd do everything he could to help me. After he finished his first serving he helped himself to another. I'd replied that I could manage then tried to retract it in case it sounded like I could manage without him. I'd asked him if he wanted me to pack his things. He'd replied that while I did that he'd ring Rita to see if she could come to pick him up. If she wasn't able to he'd ask his new manager, Pete, to help him.

Pete was staying the spare room at the back of our house. Steve'd told me that he and Pete had everything organised. Pete'd help out with the rent until I'd got myself together. Steve'd added he'd taken all the money from our joint bank account to put it down as a deposit on his new band equipment. He didn't know about my second bank account. The one that was mine. It'd kick start our new life.

'The kids want to say goodnight to you, Jenny.'

Steve placed his arms lovingly around Rita.

'Would you make the coffee, Rita? I won't be long.'

I'd asked Pete why he didn't tell me what was going on. He'd looked a bit shame-faced and said it was because Steve had so many other women on a promise he didn't think it'd go as far as it did. He also told me it was worse when you got thrown out the way he'd been by his wife.

I walked into the kids' bedroom and sat down on the edge of the bed. They looked so tiny, and also something I hadn't seen before—they looked scared. Had I been that bad?

'Did you have a good time today?'

'We had a picnic and Daddy took us to the zoo.'

Gemma spoke on behalf of Rosie.

Rosie smiled.

'Can we give Rita the clouds?'

'Sure you can.'

I bent over to give both of them a kiss.

'We don't love you anymore,' Gemma told me. 'You're a bitch. We only love Rita and Daddy.'

She pushed me away.

Don't react, I told myself, don't react.

'I have to go now,' I told the children as I pulled the bedcovers up on both of them.

'I want to talk to Daddy and Rita, ok?' I kissed them both goodnight.

'Can Rita come in and kiss us goodnight too?' Rosie asked.

'Of course.'

'We don't want you,' Gemma added. 'You're a selfish bitch.'

'I'll ask Rita to come in.'

"Just be grateful," Pete'd said, "that you're still young enough to piece your life together."

"I was born old," I'd replied. "I'd be grateful just to feel young for once."

"He didn't think it through," Pete'd said. "I'm sure he didn't mean to embarrass you."

"Yair he did. He was beyond fury when my story got published."

"It came as a bit of a shock to him that's all," Pete'd replied. "He didn't think you'd amount to anything. I mean none of us did. Steve is the one who's loaded with talent."

'Rita? The kids want to say goodnight to you.'

'Ok. The coffee's made.'

Rita gave Steve a light kiss on the head as she made her way to the kids' bedroom.

'The kids really like Rita, Jen,' Steve said as he stirred sugar into his coffee. 'They get on really well. What do you think of her?'

'She seems really nice.'

'She's very like you in a lot of ways—you know—really independent—a bit of a feminist. She has a lot of opinions of her own.'

'I noticed that.'

Please make her last until I get the kids and me thousands of miles away from here so there's no going back.

'She'd be a good person to show your writing to. She could give you really great criticism.'

He put his teaspoon onto my typewriter. It began to drip coffee into the keys. It was all I could do not to scream. I picked the spoon up and flicked it into the kitchen sink.

'At least you don't have to worry about me anymore. Pete can do that. I mean I know you want to write more stuff but I think you will really struggle to follow that last story up. I know it's hard for you but seriously you'll need to wait until the kids grow up and leave home to do any more writing quite frankly.'

And go on the aged pension.

'Would you like some toast?'

I have to stop feeding him.

'Thanks. I'm sure when you get to know Rita better you'll be really good friends.'

Good bloody grief. What else is there to say?

'Do you want some jam on it?'

I held the butter knife over the jam jar.

'Yeah. What did you want to talk about anyway?'

'I've had to quit my job because I don't have anyone to mind the children at night since you moved out. I approached social security for help. They told me that Pete has to move out.'

'What? What for?'

'He's a potential boyfriend. If he doesn't go by the end of the week, they'll won't pay any benefits.'

I've always paid my own way before but I have to go through the motions.

'Jesus Christ! How will you manage?'

'I felt like a whore when that man from the Department started to poke around in everything then asked really personal questions.'

'That's not on. I'll go and see them and tell them that it's just not on.'

For a moment I thought he was defending my virtue so I began to say how grateful I was but he cut me off before I got very far.

'Jesus Christ—you and Pete? They have to be joking. He's got five other chicks that I know of. He'd hardly be after you. Have you seen that African one he's got?'

'She came around yesterday.'

'How that guy has got the strength to keep it up I don't know. What'd Pete say about it anyway?'

'He told them he'd swear out a statutory declaration stating that he has never slept with me, and never will as you have pointed out and he is currently looking for somewhere else to live.'

'That's good. But having to pay all the rent by yourself will be a problem, especially as you've had to quit work. Perhaps you can get another deserted wife or single parent in or try to get more work during the day? There must be something you can think of.'

Steve'd begun to laugh as if he had just heard the funniest joke in his life.

'It's not funny.'

'It is when you think about it. As if Pete would go off with you. What a joke. Hey Rita, did you hear that?'

'Coming.'

'Social Security has told Pete to get out because he might end up sleeping with Jenny.'

Rita sat down and Steve took her hand in his.

'He wouldn't do that. He's too nice.'

'Does he help you out much, Jen?'

'He talks to me a lot. Mainly lectures.'

I think he's making passes at me but they're so discrete I can't tell whether they are or not. I don't want any more of this shit. Why do men always line up for sex when you break up with someone?

'I think he thinks I might commit suicide.'

'Yeah right.'

Steve snorted again.

'Sometimes I think it's the only thing I've got left that you haven't taken.'

'I'm not putting up with this shit.'

Steve began to get up out of the chair.

'I'm sorry.'

I'll be good.

'You can't blame me for you getting hurt. You just won't let me go. I had to be tough about it. It was the only way to finish things between us. You've held me back long enough. I've got my whole life to think about not this crap.'

You could've left my money in the bank.

Stay focused, Jenny, money is only stuff.

'So do I.'

'I've told you a thousand times,' Steve rolled his eyes at Rita—see what I've got to put up with? 'It's too difficult for you to go out when the kids are so small. When they grow up, you'll be able to do lots of things. Meet people. Write again. Play piano. Compose. Whatever. Did you apply for Housing?'

'It's a five-year wait.'

I don't want to waste one more second on you or any of this shit let alone another five years.

'Well try and get another boarder or something—really it's not our problem. You have to stop hanging on to me.'

It has to be now. You have to say it now.

'Is that it? Rita and I have to go home. It's getting late.'

'I don't want to stay here anymore.'

'What?'

'I don't want to stay here anymore.'

'Why?'

'I hate Perth.'

'You're nuts. You can have a really good time in Perth.'

'I'm not.'

'Steve—I think what Jenny means—is that she finds Perth—uncultured. I think that's what you mean Jenny, isn't it?'

'Yes.'

'Where do you want to go?' Steve tried to wrap his mind around this new turn of events. 'The country? Rents are pretty cheap right out in the bush.'

'I want to go back to Sydney.'

'Don't be so stupid.'

Steve realised his meal ticket was slipping out of his grasp.

'How are you going to survive in Sydney? It's far too expensive. How will you get there? You haven't got any money?'

You could catch a whale shark with that bit of bait.
'The Red Cross will give me the air fares.'
I'm the biggest disaster they've had since Italy.
'I told them I'd pay them back.'
'When will you all be going?'
'We aren't all going—just me.'
'Wait a minute.'
'I want you to take the children.'
Please let them be alright.
'You're kidding.'
'No.'
'I'm not giving you an answer tonight.'
'Would you like some wine?'
Pete's got several casks in the fridge. I'll give them that.
'Yeah.'
'Rita?'
'Thank you.'
'Just to get it clear. It'd mean that I'd have to mind the children full-time and look after them.'
'Yes.'
'For how long exactly?'
'About two months. I'll work non-stop to get the money for a place and for the children's air fares. I'll send money to you too.'
'I'll need it. The payments on the new systems are really heavy. What do you think, Rita?'
'Well—jeeze—I dunno. I mean, they couldn't stay at our place Steve, could they? The others in the house, well, you have to understand, Jenny, we all have our own lives to lead, and the kids, well, the kids get a bit noisy. I can't help much either Steve. I'm rehearsing a new play. We're doing one about Sylvia Path. I'm playing Sylvia.'
'Two months is too long.' Steve had been calculating his options while Rita was talking. 'I suppose I could move back in here. Pete could stay and help out with the rent. You'd have to send me cash. Oh by the by, you freaked everyone out at our house the other day.'
'I'm sorry. I didn't mean to. I had to see you about the—.'
The dog. He wasn't allowed to stay on either. Temporarily I'd sent him back to our old neighbours in Melbourne.
'I hate to get heavy about it but could you just ring if you have something to say in future. It's less embarrassing for everyone all round.'
'Some more wine?'
Why am I drinking it? It'll make me sick.
'Darling,' Rita wanted to run from the change in her fortunes, 'look

at the time. I have to be at rehearsals first thing tomorrow.'

'We'll talk about this some other time Jenny.'

'I have to know now.'

'It's not convenient now. You can't just dump this on us and expect an answer straight away.'

'I can go home by myself Steve.' Rita turned to me. 'We have a lot of hassles too you know, Jenny. You're not the only one. I've got a problem with my director.'

'Will you be alright by yourself Rita?'

'I've made up my mind, Steve. Anyone who doesn't like what we're doing can go to hell. I don't need them.'

They're perfect for each other—at a pinch, for at least six weeks.

'Thank you for coming, Rita.'

'That's cool. I hope things work out for you Jenny I really do.'

'I'll see you to the car, Rita. I'll be back in a minute, Jenny.'

What's taking him so long? It feels like hours.

'Would you like another drink, Steve?'

'Ta. We'll mind the kids for you Jenny, but two months is far too long. Rita has a new play to work on, and I have to get the band on the road soon. You'll have to get the money together say, inside a month. It's all the time we can spare.'

'I'm really sorry things turned out like this. But it's for the best. Will you be alright in Sydney by yourself?'

'Yes.'

Please let the kids be okay.

'Where will you stay?'

'With John and Philippe.'

Please let the kids be okay.

'They still together? You know, just sitting here with you like this—it's funny. I feel like folding you up in my arms and never letting you go.'

'Why don't you?'

'Well—because I can't.'

'Why not?'

This is ridiculous.

'Well—because I—well—it's because I promised Rita I wouldn't.'

Oh right.

'When are you thinking of leaving?'

'Wednesday.'

'I didn't realise it would be so soon. I'd better be going. I have to do a concert for Aboriginal Land Rights tomorrow. I'd never met any blackfellas before last week. You should come along and meet some.

Those poor bastards are really getting screwed.'
I think I'm gonna to be sick. I've had too much wine.
'Goodnight.'
I am gunna be sick.
'Jenny?'
'Yes.'
'What are you doing in there? The door's locked.'
'Vomiting.'
'Why? Are you sick?'
'No. Just vomiting.'
'Oh.'
'I'll be out in a minute Pete.'
'Do you want a cup of tea?'
'No thanks. I'm going to bed.'
'Did you work things out with Steve and Rita?'
'Yes.'
'What are you going to do?'
'I'm going to Sydney on Wednesday. You can stay on here. With the kids.'
'Is that what you want?'
'It's what I've got.'
'Are you alright?'
'Yeah sure. Goodnight Pete.'
'Jenny?'
'Yes.'
'Can I come in?'
'No.'
'I'm tired Jen. Jesus Christ I'm tired.'
'Then go to bed.'
'Thanks.'
'Not in my bed. It's not big enough.'
'You're right.'
'You're drunk.'
'You're right. So are you.'
Shit.
'Put me down.'
'No.'
'You don't even look like Rhett Butler.'
'No—but ah feels like Rhett Butler.'
'I'll lose welfare.'
'Fuck welfare.'
'What about your Statutory Declaration?'

'I lied. You've got nice breasts.'

'Are you going to stop?'

You always get screwed by the manager on your way out, babe. Who said that?

'Do you like being sucked?'

'No.'

Probably the same person who told me that hope was just postponed disappointment.

'Christ your skin is soft.'

I don't care anymore. I know I should but I don't.

'Are you comfortable like that?'

'No.'

I don't care.

'It's nice isn't it?'

'No.'

'What time are you leaving?'

'On the 'red eye'.'

'What are you going to do when you get to Sydney?'

'I dunno. I'll think of something.'

###

ABOUT THE AUTHOR

The author, G. Dixon Lowndes was born in Mitchell, a small town on the edge of the Maranoa River in south-western Queensland, Australia.

The Ooline bottle trees from the remnants of a rainforest in times long ago are still there. They are currently in flower.

Her life and her award winning short stories has been informed by Mitchell.

In the highly successful television drama serial, *Neighbours*, as the writer, script and story editor, the town of Mitchell and her family became the fictitious Mitchell family—Charlene, Henry and Madge.

Mitchell again inspired her first fictional novel in the *Corrugated Roads* series. It was published by Montpelier Press in 2010. It has now been extensively re-written and is available as this e-book. It is the first instalment of a künstlerroman or the novels that tell the story of an artist's life.

The second book is *Corrugated Roads. Rollin' Down the Road. 1960s-1970s.* The next is *Corrugated Roads. Lilies on a Dustbin. 1970s-1980s.*

The author has a Master of Arts from Griffith University in 2005. She was awarded Alumnus of the Year in November 2011 by Griffith University, School of Arts, Queensland, Australia.